Slam Dunk

Steven Barwin
&
Gabriel David Tick

James Lorimer & Company, Publishers
Toronto, 1998

© 1998 Steven Barwin & Gabriel David Tick

All rights reserved. No part of this book may be reproduced or transmitted in any form or by any means, electronic or mechanical, including photocopying, or by any information storage or retrieval system, without permission in writing from the publisher.

James Lorimer & Company acknowledges the support of the Department of Canadian Heritage and the Ontario Arts Council in the development of writing and publishing in Canada. We acknowledge the support of the Canada Council for the Arts for our publishing program.

Cover illustration: Sharif Tarabay

Canadian Cataloguing in Publication Data
Barwin, Steven
   Slam Dunk
   (Sports stories)

ISBN 1-55028-599-8 (bound) ISBN 1-55028-598-X (pbk.)
I. Tick, Gabriel David. II. Title. III. Series: Sports stories (Toronto, Ont.)
PS8553.A7836S53 1998   jC813'.54   C98-930371-3
PZ7.B37Sl 1998

James Lorimer & Company Ltd., Publishers
35 Britain Street
Toronto, Ontario
M5A 1R7

Printed and bound in Canada

Contents

1	Flip Side	1
2	Slice and Dice	11
3	Ground Zero	20
4	The Big Pitch	27
5	The Hustler	35
6	Risky Business	43
7	Like It's 1999	49
8	Hang Over	57
9	Mission Impossible	65
10	Cosmic Crunch	74
11	Sub Zero	83
12	Life on Mars	86

1

Flip Side

Practice was a complete joke. Everyone was making a mad rush for the basketball with complete disregard for the rules of the game. Mason looked through the herd of players seeing guys elbowing, tripping, and even tackling each other. He thought the rough contact made the game look more like tackle football than basketball.

"You guys are crazy!" Mason yelled.

"Tell them something they don't already know," Tyrone replied as he ran his fingers through his thick curly hair. He was the only one to hear Mason over the discordant ruckus.

"The only reason they're acting like this is because Coach Pollinoffsky isn't watching," Mason said, wishing he had the coach's brawny vocal cords to bring everyone to a standstill.

Tyrone looked at Mason and said, "This is probably how people acted when the wheel was invented — everyone knocking each other out of the way so they could try it out ... watch it roll."

"Where'd you come up with that one?" Mason asked.

"My brain," Tyrone said, inspired by today's lecture in History of Civilization: "In The Beginning."

"Anyway," Mason said, "you wouldn't know that this is the last practice before the season opener."

"Should we just stand here," Tyrone continued, as a player behind him did an elegant swan dive into the hardwood, "or should we join them?"

"Let's go for it!" Mason exclaimed.

Just then, everyone laughed as Isaac tripped for no apparent reason and came to a scraping halt in front of Mason's Avivas. Mason stomped down on the basketball, freezing it under his size nines. "You okay?" he asked Isaac.

"What?" Isaac asked from behind his coke-bottle glasses.

Mason really liked Isaac. Despite the fact that Isaac had two left feet and never coordinated his sock colours, he had the best shot in the league. If he was standing still with a clear shot on net, Isaac could always swish it in. Mason thought that Isaac hid long-distance radar equipment under his thick crop of black hair.

Mason extended his right hand down to help his fallen teammate back to his feet. "Are you okay? That was a pretty bad wipe out."

Isaac dusted himself off and looked around to see everyone gawking at him. "Yeah, I've had worse."

"Are we going to play or what?" Buckley screamed at the top of his lungs. His face was plum-red from running around after the basketball. Mason didn't answer, and the basketball remained lodged under his right sneaker. He was trying to play it cool.

Buckley screamed again, "Do you wanna yak yak yak all day or play some b-ball?"

Mason knew how to handle Buckley Bernard. Buckley thought he was hip. In fact, in Mason's opinion Buckley acted as though he had achieved the acclaim of Tiger Woods. Everything from his water bottle to his cool crimson-coloured socks had the Nike logo plastered on it.

"Play." Mason barked out after a few tense beats of silence. He flipped the basketball onto the top of his right foot as though it were a soccer ball and he were Pelé. Then he flicked the basketball into his hands. He began to dribble the ball and sauntered toward centre court.

"I'm in the open any time," Tyrone said, loudly enough for only Mason to hear.

From the corner of his eye, Mason could see Tyrone a step behind him in the wing-man position. Then he focused on the red-rimmed net, rather than on the pack of hungry wolves closing in on him. Buckley was definitely the roughest in the gang of untamed wolves. If they wanted to play tackle basketball, Mason thought, then he'd better muster all his strength. He dug his left foot into the aged hardwood floor and then ploughed into the tangle of players ahead. Mason had to barrel through six of them — more than anyone would encounter in a real game.

"Get him!" Buckley busted out, sending everyone after Mason.

Thinking quickly, Mason threw the ball back to Tyrone. As Tyrone grabbed it, the attacking players changed course like a flock of birds and went after him. Afraid, Tyrone whipped the ball back to Mason, throwing it overhand like Dan Marino. Mason caught the ball and protected it within his arms as though he were a line backer for the San Francisco 49ers. He mowed through several players, ignoring the fact that he was supposed to dribble the ball. This was street rules and the coach wasn't around to call travelling, so he continued to run in his football stance. Mason looked up to see Buckley waiting for him like a big, red road block. Oh great. Push hard! he commanded his legs. Mason deked left around Buckley and jumped up at the same time because he saw Buckley stick out a leg to try and trip him. Mason cleared his opponent. He charged the net and leapt into the air to try the impossible slam dunk —

"Wahhhhhhh!" The coach's whistle blew, causing everyone to freeze in their tracks.

Mason was in mid-flight so he decided to toss the ball up as he came crashing down to earth. Everyone watched as the ball bounced off the top of the backboard, then down off the rim to the ground.

"So close," Mason said to anyone in earshot.

"So that's how you want to play this season," Coach Pollinoffsky said. "Like a bunch of orangutans."

"Figures that I'm the one to get caught," Mason grumbled to Buckley. Buckley sneered at him.

Everyone gathered in a semi-circle around the coach. Some of the shorter guys struggled to see the coach, who reminded Mason of a grumpy Danny DeVito. He was short, stout, wore a combover hairdo, and had a stern smile.

"Okay, men," the coach said as though he were a commander talking to his foot soldiers. "I've got some good news and some bad news about this season."

Murmuring and muttering spread through the guys like wildfire through dry brush. Everyone knew that that was one of the most ominous ways of starting a sentence.

It's like starting a sentence with "You better sit down for this ..." Mason chuckled to himself.

"Give us the bad news, first," Buckley called out.

"Okay." Coach Pollinoffsky cleared his throat, "We don't have enough players to partake in the regular school season league this year."

"That's impossible," Tyrone belted.

"Well, I just found out from the drama department that four of you — you know who you are — have been cast in this year's play, *Fiddler on the Roof*."

"I don't believe it," Mason groaned. He didn't want the guys who made the play to see that he was angry. But deep down he was.

The guys who made the theatre troupe huddled around and congratulated each other.

"I think we all owe the fine young thespians who were cast in *Fiddler* a big round of applause."

Everyone forced their applause for the sake of the coach. The entire team looked let down.

"So what are we going to do?" Tyrone asked.

"Yeah, what's the good news?" Isaac added.

Coach Pollinoffsky looked up at the remnants of the basketball team he had so carefully chosen. "The good news is that I have found some players to replace them."

The fragmented team looked around at each other, wondering if the coach was going to pluck a crop of digitized players from the school's computer database.

Mason asked what was on everyone's mind, "What's the catch?"

Coach Pollinoffsky cleared his throat again and said, "To get the players we need, the Cabbagetown Raptors are going to go co-ed."

Buckley asked, "What are you talking about?"

But Buckley knew exactly what the coach was talking about.

"League rules state that all teams have the option of being co-ed," the coach said. "I think it's a great idea. We get the players we need. *And* we turn a new page in the Raptors' history. Girls are going to be a great addition to the team. Trust me."

Mason looked around, sensing there wasn't a lot of trust in this bunch right now.

Receiving no positive feedback, the coach continued, "The Raptors have never missed a season since they started playing basketball here in 1933. I've found five wonderfully talented young players who have expressed a strong interest in playing with us. In fact, from now on I'm opening the team try-outs to both men and women."

The guys took in the coach's speech.

"I think it's a cool idea!" Isaac said, wanting to be the first to jump on board the new and improved Raptors organization. But not everyone was convinced that turning co-ed was the way to go.

"I think it sucks," Buckley said.

Mason wasn't against the idea. But he wouldn't be completely on board until he got a chance to see the girls play.

"Another incentive to welcome the girls onto our team is that if we do well this year, the national finals are going to be held in Ottawa." The coach offered this hoping to hammer the last spike into the idea of a fresh and enriched Raptors team.

"Let's give it a try," Mason said. Mason's best friend Brent had moved to Ottawa in September, and ever since Mason had been dying to go and hang out with him. If the Raptors didn't make the finals there was little chance Mason would see Brent ... probably before the end of the century.

The coach took a step back and announced, "Here are your new teammates." As if on cue, the five girls came out from their locker room and clumped together on one side of the coach. The boys stayed on the other side.

Coach Pollinoffsky said, "Guys, here are Cindy, Nikki, Anita, Juliana, and Erin."

The guys looked at each other; the girls looked at each other. All in complete silence. Mason locked his eyes on a splinter of wood in the floor.

For the first time since Mason could remember the gymnasium was dead quiet. You could hear a pin drop.

The coach must have been able to feel the air of tension as well. "So ..." he searched for the right words. "So let's take a practice. We're really under the gun here guys ..." the coach realized he had left out the other half, "... and girls."

"This is gonna be interesting," Tyrone whispered to Mason.

Mason answered, "If you want to go to Ottawa, keep an open mind."

"Unfortunately this is our last opportunity to practise before the season opener on October twenty-eighth," said the coach. He picked up a basketball. "Let's give it a try. I'll divide everyone up, so both sides have girls and guys."

Mason took his position at centre court for the tip off. He watched as, if he remembered correctly, Cindy walked passed him. Her long hair was pulled back into a clip and her ear to ear smile made her look really friendly.

"Hi, my name's Cindy," she said.

"I'm *Hason*," Mason replied nervously.

She laughed and then said, "*Hason*? I've never heard that name before."

"I mean *M*ason," he corrected himself, going red with embarrassment. He wondered why he was so nervous.

Coach Pollinoffsky blew his whistle, sending a sharp shriek into the air. He tossed the ball sky high, between Mason and Nikki.

Mason reached the ball with the tips of his fingers at the same time as Nikki. With her long legs she's a great jumper he thought to himself in mid-air. He managed to get a bit of extra mustard on the ball and knocked it sideways to Cindy. As Mason touched down, Buckley cut into Cindy and grabbed the ball from her.

"I don't need any heroes," Coach Pollinoffsky yelled while clapping his hands for encouragement.

Buckley ran with the ball, saw Anita in the open, but deliberately passed to Isaac.

"You know things are bad when Buckley's passing to Isaac. They hate each other," Mason said to Tyrone.

Mason and Tyrone watched Isaac catch the ball, plant his feet firmly on the ground, and nail the shot from the three-point line.

Tyrone grabbed the bouncing ball, took it to the base line and began to stride toward the oppositions' end.

Mason signalled that he was ready for the pass. He snatched the feed from Tyrone and quickly passed deep, in Cindy's direction. She took the pass and made an aggressive move toward the basket.

In the key, Buckley tried to trip Cindy just as he had tried to trip Mason earlier. But Cindy managed to shift her weight so she could pass the ball.

Mason got in the open, but decided not to call for the pass. He wanted to see what she could do on the court. Cindy tossed the ball at the backboard with enough backspin that it dunked in.

"Cool shot," Mason said to Tyrone.

"Yeah, she's really good."

Despite the great shot, Mason saw nobody congratulate Cindy. He turned to Tyrone and commented, "Did you see Buckley and the other guys? They're not playing with the girls at all."

Tyrone said, "Yeah, but I bet if they did, we'd do really well."

Mason wanted to go over and high-five Cindy, but he felt uncomfortable doing that with someone he had just met ... not to mention he was still embarrassed about the Hason thing.

"Come on guys and girls," the coach yelled. "First game's just around the corner and if we play like this we're never going to make it anywhere."

But Mason could see that the coach's plea fell on deaf ears. Mason hoped the practice would pick up. Half his mind was on winning a trophy and having fun, the other half was on going to Ottawa.

Unfortunately, the rest of the practice was awful. Everyone was dreading the first game of the season.

* * * * *

At home, Mason's mom punched into the phone what seemed to Mason an infinite sequence of numbers, which they had to use for their long-distance calling plan. Finally she handed him the phone and said, "Ten minutes, okay?"

"Yeah, ten," Mason agreed, expecting his mom to pull out a stopwatch. "Are you serious?" he exclaimed as he watched his mom set "ten minutes" on the microwave timer. What's this, sudden-death overtime? he wondered. Then he heard Brent say, "No way, what?"

Mason realized that Brent thought he was talking to him. "No, I was talking to my mom."

"What do you mean?" Brent queried.

This is not how I pictured spending the only time I get to talk to my best friend, Mason thought. "Forget it, man." Mason wanted to make the most of his twenty cents a minute. "So what's up?"

"Ottawa's cold. But I got to see a Senators game."

"Don't even try to compare Ottawa to Toronto ... we have the Leafs, Raptors, Blue Jays, and Argos. This is sports heaven," Mason said, trying to protect his city from any geographical rivalry.

"Yeah, but I'm living minutes from the Ottawa arena."

"I don't believe you," Mason said. "I've always wanted to live across the street from Maple Leaf Gardens."

He heard Brent and even though he was three hundred clicks away he sounded like he was next door.

"And in November the CANAL freezes over!" said Brent excitedly. "I can skate all the way downtown."

"That's so cool. We don't have anything like that here."

Five minutes later, the microwave counted down to zero and Mason said goodbye and hung up the phone. He had excited thoughts of hanging out with his long-distance best friend in Canada's capital.

2

Slice and Dice

As Mason angled the corner of Parliament and Struther Street he could see a group of his friends hanging around the school's outdoor basketball court. It was their fall ritual. Before the weather got really bad, the gang liked to chill out before the 9 a.m. bell. It was one of Mason's favourite parts of the day. He would get up twenty minutes earlier than he normally did so that he wouldn't miss it. They'd all sit around the green, splintery bleachers and talk. Sometimes they'd help each other with homework due later that day. Other times they'd cram for tests.

It was an exceptionally beautiful morning and Mason couldn't help but notice that the trees were starting to turn colour. Some were transforming into a light green while others were already slightly yellowish. Mason knew that soon they'd be flaming red, deep orange, and lush purple. The summer had sped by so fast that he couldn't believe fall was already here. After summer, fall was his second-favourite time of year. The air wasn't too hot or too cold, so he could play any outdoor sport he wanted to without worrying about freezing his ears off.

As Mason got closer to the guys he could see that something was wrong. They looked mad. Rodney, a square-jawed, curly haired guy who was usually the class clown, paced back and forth in front of the other guys while staring at the basketball court. He had a real serious look on his face. Isaac, Buckley, Gavin, and Tyrone just sat there — each looking more distressed than the other.

"What's going on, guys?" Mason asked as he dropped his knapsack on the splintery wooden bleachers.

"What do you mean, what's wrong?" Rodney shot back. "Having girls on the team is going to mess everything up."

"Yeah," Buckley agreed as he laced up his new pair of fancy cross-trainers, which were always coming undone.

Mason grabbed a seat beside Tyrone.

"The Raptors have never had girls on the team before. Why start now?" Rodney continued, "We're going to be the laughing stock of the entire city."

"I remember when Central Tech had a girl on their basketball team," Buckley said. "They didn't win a single game."

Mason thought about what they were saying and it didn't sit well with him. If the team lost more than one game they wouldn't be able to go to Ottawa and he wouldn't get to see Brent. But without the girls on the team there wouldn't be enough players to make them eligible to play in the league.

"We need the girls," Mason said. "Without them we don't have a team."

"I don't know if I want to play," Isaac said as he gazed through his thick glasses at a bunch of baby crows that were hopping around the basketball court. "I mean, what's the point."

"The point is that we should at least try. Maybe we can actually win." Mason continued, "Then we get to go to Ottawa to play in the nationals."

"And get laughed at by the whole country," Buckley spat. "No thanks."

Mason didn't want girls on the team any more than the other guys did. There were sixty-five years of school tradition being challenged here. Cabbagetown Junior High had never mixed their teams. But he didn't understand why the guys would be embarrassed. It was the nineties. More and more co-ed teams were popping up all over the place. Even the NHL had had a woman goaltender. "What if the girls turn out to be really great players?" Mason asked. "Cindy and Nikki played well at practice yesterday."

"I agree," Tyrone piped in. "They could be great. My aunt Debra played for the Canadian National team. They beat almost everybody. She even went to the Soeul Olympics."

"Maybe she should play for us then," Gavin joked.

Although yesterday's practice hadn't gone well at all, Mason thought the girls had solid shooting skills — and that's what the team needed.

"I'm definitely not playing. I'm off the team," Buckley stated as if he had just come to a decision.

"Yeah, me too," Rodney agreed.

This was not good, Mason thought. In fact, it was bad. "Come on, guys," he said. "Don't give up before the season even starts."

Rodney stopped staring at the court for a second and looked Mason right in the eyes. "Get off it, Ashbury."

Mason wasn't going to back down. "I think you're just afraid," he said. "We've been playing basketball together since elementary school. Just because things are changing a little bit doesn't mean we have to stop playing together."

Tyrone stood up. "He's got a point."

With that, the five minute warning buzzer sounded and the guys grabbed their school bags and headed indoors.

"This isn't over," Rodney promised.

* * * * *

Mason hurried down the lime-green school hallway at a pace just short of a run. Biology class was about to start and today they were going to dissect frogs.

"Slow down, Mason," Ms. Chan warned as Mason hustled past her.

That was the last thing he wanted to hear. If he didn't get to class soon he wouldn't get a good partner. The last thing he wanted was to dissect a frog with someone he didn't get along with. He preferred to do these types of projects with his friends. After all, when he was young he, Brent, and Gavin used to go down to Birchside Park and catch frogs. They'd wade into the mucky swamps beneath the big maple tree with a mesh net, waiting patiently for just the right moment. Then, SWOOSH. They would swing their nets around and scoop up a frog as it jumped from one lily pad to another. At the end of the day they would release the frogs back to the wild. They mostly enjoyed the fun of pretending to hunt. But that was a long time ago. Now, Mason had more urgent problems to think about ... like getting to biology class.

"Sorry, Ms. Chan. I'll walk slower," Mason said as he continued down the locker-lined hallway.

It seemed like forever but he finally got there. This was the first time that class was being held in the laboratory. There were four rows of long, black, waist-high counters. In the front of the room there was a skeleton with a big white name tag stuck to its rib cage that read "Bernie." Bernie stood next to the blackboard, watching over the class. In front of the blackboard was a short, black podium that Mr. Takei, the biology teacher, was standing behind.

Mason scanned the room for a spot. It looked like everything was taken. Everyone appeared to paired off. Tyrone and Gavin were perched at the back of the room. Buckley and

Rodney were at the counter in front of them. Mason couldn't believe his bad luck.

"Mason," Mr. Takei said while pointing, "why don't you go stand with Cindy over there. Neither of you has a partner."

That sucked, Mason thought. Not only was he not going to be with one of his friends but he was stuck dissecting a frog with a girl. And not just any girl, but a girl that he immediately recognized as being on his basketball team.

Mason ambled over to the bench and flumped his knapsack down. He tried his best not to look at Cindy. He thought that if he kept his distance he might get through the class without talking to her.

"Hi, Hason. Oops, I mean, Mason," she said with a smile.

Well, so much for that plan. "Hi Cindy," he said as he turned to make eye contact with her. To his astonishment she looked as friendly as he had remembered her from the practice. From rows behind him, Mason could hear his buddies laughing at him.

"So, have you ever dissected a frog before?" Cindy asked.

"Well, I used to catch them in the park and then let them go."

"Me too." Cindy said. "My friends and I used to go to —"

Mason cut her off. "Birchside Park?"

"Yeah, how did you know?" she asked, amazed that Mason was following her train of thought.

"We used to go there, too. I loved stomping around in the muck, letting it squish between my toes," Mason said, thinking it was cool that they had something in common.

Mr. Takei went into the back room and wheeled out a shiny metallic stand that had seven extra-large pickle jars resting on it. In each jar Mason could see several greenish-grey frogs, floating around in the formaldehyde. "Now," Mr. Takei said, "I want one person from each group to get the instruments for the dissection and the other to come over to me and pick up your frog."

Mason and Cindy looked at each other, knowing that they both wanted to retrieve the frog.

"Do you want to get the frog?" Mason asked, hoping her answer would be no.

"Thanks," Cindy said as she took off for the front of the room.

Mason made his way to the supply table. He reached for a scalpel which had a tightly sealed safety cap on it. Then he took a pair of giant tweezers, five glass petri dishes, a small board that had a pin stuck in each of its four corners, and a long piece of string. The instruments of a typical mad scientiest, Mason chuckled to himself.

When he got back to the bench, Cindy had already returned with the lifeless frog. It stunk, Mason thought, but didn't want to lose his cool in front of Cindy. He didn't remember frogs smelling that bad at Birchside Park.

"Oooh, it smells," Cindy observed.

"It smells like ... like dirty socks," Mason said to her.

"Exactly," she agreed. "Mixed with the smell of old bicycle-tire inner tubes."

Mr. Takei got up in front of everyone to officially start the class. "You're probably wondering why the subjects smell so awful," he said.

Mason laughed quietly. He always thought it was funny that science teachers never referred to things as they really were. Why couldn't Mr. Takei just call the *subject* a dead frog.

The teacher continued talking. "All the blood is drained out of them and they are kept pickled in formaldehyde."

Mason had never eaten a pickle that smelled this bad.

Everyone in the class concentrated as Mr. Takei walked them though the dissection procedure. First, they were to lay the frog down on its back on the small board. Then they would take each of the frog's limbs and tie them to their respective corner so the frog would be spread-eagle.

Once Mr. Takei finished discussing the process everyone got to work. After a while Mason didn't mind working with Cindy. He realized he was actually having fun with her.

Cindy took the scalpel and made the first incision from just below the frog's chin to the bottom of its belly. Mason looked on, watching every move.

"Scalpel," Mason ordered as though he were one of those doctors on TV and the frog's life depended on it.

Cindy passed him the scalpel and he made the next incision directly across the width of the frog.

"Cool," said Mason.

"Yeah, it's really neat," Cindy agreed as she took the tweezers and peeled back the frog's skin.

They both looked on in amazement as the frog's inner workings were exposed. They could see the heart, the lungs, the stomach, and the liver.

Each organ was a different colour. The lungs were blue — but not a normal ocean blue, Mason noted. They were as blue as extremely ripe blueberries.

"That's the heart," Cindy said as she directed Mason's gaze to a dark red glob.

"It doesn't look like a heart," Mason said as he got one of the petri dishes ready.

Cindy skillfully cut around the heart and extracted it from the frog's body.

Mason took the tweezers and placed the heart in the dish. "It kind of looks like a weird snail," he observed.

"Or a piece of a torn-up basketball," Cindy said.

Mason had been hoping that the word "basketball" wouldn't come up at all. "It *could* look like that," he mumbled, hoping that Cindy's mind would drift from anything to do with basketball.

"So, how do you think the team's going to do this year?" she asked.

Oh, great. Now the topic of conversation was stuck on the harmless subject of basketball. He wasn't sure how honest to be about the team's dim chances. "We'll do okay," he said.

"We were really nervous to come and play on the boys' team. Some of the girls actually didn't want to do it."

Mason was taken aback. He had never considered that there was another side to the story. It was a given that the boys didn't want the girls on the team. But he hadn't for a moment thought that the girls might not want to be on the boys' team. "Why wouldn't you want to play with us?" Mason asked.

"We have our own league. And we've won the championship for two years in a row. But if our best players are playing on your team, chances are the girls' team won't win."

"I see what you mean. None of the guys really want girls on the team. But we don't have enough players to play in the league without you."

"Do you think we can win?" Cindy asked.

"I think we'll do okay if we play together. We've definitely got the talent. It's just a matter of being able to use it."

"I agree," Cindy muttered as she dug in behind the frog's lungs. Mason held the skin back with the tweezers and watched his partner make incisions to remove the organ.

"We'll see what happens tomorrow night. First games are always really tough. The York Mills Rockets are a very good team."

"That's just the beginning, because there are even better teams out there," Cindy remarked.

He gave her the tweezers in exchange for the scalpel. Then he made a slight incision at the base of the frog's stomach to begin the removal of the intestine and stomach. Mason's mind was not on the frog project. His brain raced with the daunting thought that the Raptors could only afford to lose one game. Anymore than that, Mason figured, and there was no way he was going to get a free trip to see Brent.

"Watch what you're doing!" Cindy exclaimed.

Mason looked down and realized that he had cut too deep with the scalpel.

Cindy said, "We're gonna lose marks for that one."

"Sorry about that," Mason said.

Cindy looked behind her and then said to Mason, "The teacher's coming around to check out everyone's frog."

"I'll fix it quickly," Mason replied. But, he knew that basketball was bouncing around on his brain. He couldn't concentrate. Besides only being able to eat, sleep, and dream about b-ball, he was also nervous about being around Cindy.

As the teacher approached, Cindy engaged in some small talk to give Mason that extra second he may have needed to patch up the frog.

"It's ready!" Mason said. As he held up the tray to show the teacher it slipped from his hands. The tray crashed down and the frog ejected on impact. Mason could imagine the headline in the school's newspaper: "Star Athlete Fumbles Frog and Fails!"

3

Ground Zero

The ref tossed the ball into the air and ... the tip off. Tyrone got a fingernail on it and flicked it back into Raptor territory. From there, Cindy got a grip on it and started to dribble up court. Buckley, with shoelaces undone, ran just outside the York Mills Rockets' key as Cindy continued up court. Mason was flanking to her right.

"Pass the ball," Buckley yelled.

Just then, three Rocket players surrounded Cindy and she was locked into a defensive pyramid.

It seemed to Mason that passing wasn't an option for her. If she let go of the ball it looked like one of the Rockets would definitely get a hand on it.

"Pass it," Buckley yelled again from his prime position near their opponents' net.

Mason decided to challenge a few of the Rocket players to ease the pressure from Cindy. He ran up to the three-point mark and tried to attract their attention long enough for Cindy to make a break for it. "Hey, pass it over here," Mason screamed. It worked like magic. Two of the Rockets looked over at him as Cindy drove around the third.

She got Buckley in her cross hairs and passed the ball in his direction. But one of the Rocket defencemen got a handle on the ball and took control of it. The Rocket-man whisked it off into Raptor territory.

Anita was standing defense when the Rocket player made an aggressive move to the net. But even her lanky height couldn't stop the determined player. He climbed above her and sank a picture-perfect bucket. The buzzer went and all five Raptors scrambled off the court to the bench.

Coach Pollinoffsky stood waiting. "Everyone's playing really well."

Mason looked at the players. Too bad none of them believed that they were, he thought.

"And great try, Cindy. You did a good job getting around those players. Now, it's the end of the first quarter and we're only down by six. As far as I'm concerned it's anyone's game." The coach turned his attention to his play book.

Mason observed the team like a fighter pilot scanning the horizon. Everyone looked hot and exhausted. It was as if they had been running around in a steamy sauna. The temperature in the York Mills gym was staggering. The players were sweating profusely and the game was only fifteen minutes old. But the Rockets were suffering under the same conditions, so it wasn't exactly unfair.

Mason liked it hot. In the summer he loved shooting hoops out in the blazing heat. He'd spend hours on end running up and down any one of the half-dozen neighbourhood courts, challenging anyone to a pickup game. Outside of basketball, he was also a pro at roller hockey. He remembered taking off his helmet after an especially rigorous game. The sweat had poured down his face like a water fall. So a broken thermostat in a North York gymnasium was not going to stop him from playing his best.

"Buckley," the coach announced, "you were playing well out there. But you've gotta go get the ball rather than wait for it to come to you."

Mason could see that Buckley was upset by the coach's constructive criticism.

"Well, if people could pass I might have had a basket," he protested.

It was obvious that he was referring to Cindy.

The coach retorted, "You put in a great effort. But the situation required more than just positioning."

Mason was mad that Buckley was directing his anger at Cindy. Like it was her fault that she was pegged in by three enemy players.

"Anyway, all I'm saying is that we've got to try and push for more team work," the coach said. "Now get out there."

With that, Mason, Tyrone, Buckley, Anita, and Cindy returned to the court.

As Mason trotted past Cindy, he saw Buckley give her an unfriendly shove.

The heat in the gym seemed to intensify as the game plodded sluggishly forward.

Mason thought the air felt thick as paste.

For the entire Cabbagetown team it seemed that each minute was an eternity. North York was scoring basket after basket and Cabbagetown could barely hold themselves together.

"Shoot the ball," Mason hollered at Tyrone, who was practically right under the net. But before Tyrone got the shot off a Rocket came up from behind him and stole the ball.

Mason darted toward the Rocket, tracking him all the way down court. As the Rocket took his shot Mason threw his weight into the air and snatched the ball. Quicker than swift he whizzed a pass cross-court to Buckley.

Buckley dribbled up court, a man in full command. But, as luck would have it, he was soon surrounded by a wall of Rocket players.

"Over here," Cindy hollered. She was an easy pass for Buckley and no one was guarding her.

Mason saw Buckley glance over in Cindy's direction. But instead of passing as he should have, Buckley tried to take the shot. He released the ball from the lower east side ... it rattled off the backboard into no-man's land. If there was such a thing as a five-pointer, Mason thought Buckley would definitely have deserved one if his shot had gone in. Instead, the ball flew into the stands and slammed into an unsuspecting Rocket supporter.

Mason's mother, Patricia, and her boyfriend, Jim, let out a collective "Ouch," happy that they were clear of the misguided shot.

As the game clock continued to trickle down, Mason could feel the trip to Ottawa becoming more and more unlikely. If the Raptors lost this game they would have to win every other league game that they played. Which, as anyone who'd ever played in the Toronto junior-high basketball league would tell you, was impossible. Every team lost a few — even the best. Mason wondered why coach Pollinoffsky couldn't at least put one line of just guys on the court. Maybe that would help kick-start some momentum. After all, they had enough guys for one shift. Gavin, Tyrone, Buckley, Rodney, and Mason could be a truly dynamic line. Maybe even good enough to even out the losing situation the Raptors now faced. But Mason knew that coach Pollinoffsky couldn't bench the girls.

It was the start of the second half and the scoreboard read 32 to 21 for the Rockets ... the Raptors were down by eleven. Even worse, the Raptors' morale was at an all-time low. While all the guys were blaming the girls, Mason suspected that the girls were questioning whether they really wanted to be Raptors.

Mason thought that despite this game, he'd better do his best to make the most of the situation. Turn lemons into lemonade, his mom would say. And if he didn't make lemonade, the Raptors would definitely be left high and dry.

Cindy got a hold of the ball and drove up court. There wasn't a Rocket player in sight.

Mason ran ahead of her to dig himself a good position in enemy territory.

"Over here," Buckley screamed.

Cindy glanced over to him, his hands waving in desperation. But he was well-covered by Rocket players. There was no way she could feed him the ball. So, to Buckley's disappointment, Cindy kept driving forward.

Mason saw an opportunity and stepped into the Rockets' key, establishing himself for a pass.

The shot clock began its countdown, like a ticking bomb.

Cindy saw that he was wide open, threw him a look, then made what looked like a shot on net. Mason got her telepathic message and leapt toward the net. ALLEY-OOP! Mason tipped in a two pointer.

The Raptor bench went crazy.

"Way to play together," the coach yelled. "Let's keep it going."

Now the Rockets had possession. Their guard bounced the ball a few times and chucked it over to their left forward.

This guy looks really menacing, Mason observed. The forward had long hair pulled back in a ponytail, and he was skyscraper tall. "Definitely one of the biggest players in the league," Mason relayed to Cindy.

No one had even dared to try and block the guy. He could pretty well walk right into the Raptor zone and do as he pleased.

Mason saw him going right toward Anita. So he fell back to provide more defense. The big Rocket player was in a prime position to nail a bucket.

Just then, Anita ran up to him and started to block him. She was the only one brave enough to go face-to-shoulder with him. Not only was she blocking him but she was trying to knock the ball out of his hands. But the skyscraper was too skilled to just let her grab it. Anita tried again. She aggressively swung her hands around the player and finally got a piece of the ball. It rolled out of his bear-paw hands and into the open.

FOUL. The ref's whistle blared.

With that the big Rocket took two free shots on the Raptors' net and nailed them both.

"Nice going," Buckley muttered under his breath.

Anita must have heard it because she shot him a really fierce glare. "At least I tried," she shot back.

Buckley didn't say another word.

Mason could feel the tension between the guys and girls grow more intense, but he couldn't help thinking of Cindy. They had pulled off a pretty good move earlier in the game. If everyone worked together that way, Mason thought, then they would at least be contenders. But that wasn't happening. Except for Mason and Cindy none of the guys and girls were talking to each other, let alone passing to each other.

The third and fourth quarters flew by. The Raptors got in a few lucky baskets — while the Rockets swooshed down several well-executed plays.

Mason watched the game clock as it counted down from twenty seconds. There was not even an outside chance that the Raptors would tie the game. Unless, of course, they could score twenty points in ten seconds. Not even the best players in the NBA could pull that one off.

BUZZ. That was it. The Raptors had just lost the only game they could afford to lose if they wanted to play in the nationals.

As the team shuffled out of the boiling-hot arena, Mason heard the guys complaining about the girls.

"Hey, Mason." He turned his head to see Cindy running toward him.

"Hey, Cindy. Great pass earlier in the game."

"Yeah. It was right in the zone. So, I was wondering what you're doing tomorrow night?" she asked.

"Nothing really, why?"

"I just wanted to know if you wanted to … you know, go out?"

"Sure," he said, unable to mask his grin. He could feel his heart start to beat louder and louder.

Mason just stood there, flabbergasted, as Cindy walked to the locker room. Was he dreaming or had she just asked him out on a date?

4

The Big Pitch

"How come you didn't tell me you were going out on a big date?" Mason's mom asked from behind the cash register in her convenience store.

Mason surveyed the aisle looking for a gift or at least something fun for Cindy. "It's not a date, Mom," he said, trying to get the story straight. All he needed were rumours spreading through the Ashbury clan, Mason thought. Then he'd never hear the end of it.

Mason's mom said, "Why don't you pick out something nice from the store for ... What's her name?"

"Cindy," Mason replied. He rummaged through a bin of old toys that his mom was trying to sell off. She called them "extra value gifts." Toys are a dumb idea, he said to himself. What was he thinking? If he showed up with a Slinky or Silly Putty she'd think he was the biggest loser around.

Patricia peered around the counter, wondering which aisle her son was in. "Honey, pick out anything in the store you want to give her."

Mason turned to the convex mirror in the front corner of the store. He could see his mother at the back behind the counter. "Anything I want?" Mason questioned.

"Sure, it's a special night."

He asked, "Do I have to work it off?" wondering if there was a catch.

Mason saw his mom look at him through the security mirror. "You don't have to work it off. Not this time."

So, then why was he looking in the discount bin? Mason wondered. He picked up a handful of the dirty, outdated toys and dumped them back into the bin. He said, "Thanks, Mom," and then turned his attention to the bounty of regularly priced merchandise. He cruised up and down the aisles, his eyes darting from toothpaste to magazines to vitamins to deodorant. He figured he'd better make the most of it. It wasn't every day he scored free merchandise. Thinking about that reminded him of how Brent used to always say that Mason was the luckiest person because his mom owned a convenience store. He tried to explain to Brent that he couldn't just take cartons full of anything he wanted, anytime he wanted. But Brent had it in his mind that Mason could gorge on candy anytime he craved it. He continued to scour the shelves, waiting for something to catch his eye. "That's it!" Mason blurted. He darted to the large candy section and picked out the perfect gift for his date with Cindy.

* * * * *

The giant neon light sabre swung down from Luke Skywalker's hand like a pendulum, keeping time like a metronome. "The key to mini golf is to get the timing straight in your mind," Mason said to Cindy, "and then close your eyes before hitting the golf ball."

Cindy turned to Mason, tried to keep a straight face and said, "You mean I should try to use the force?"

Mason laughed and accidentally knocked his blue ball with his putter. "You're just trying to distract me so you'll win." Then he ran down the side of the tenth hole to retrieve his ball from the bushes.

"No, I'm not," Cindy said. "By the way, that one counts as a stroke."

"No way. That was an accident." Mason placed the dimpled ball back on the white spot and began to focus on the shot. But he found it hard to concentrate on winning the game because he was having so much fun with Cindy.

"This is the most fun I've ever had playing mini golf," Cindy announced.

"I can't believe you've never been to this course before," Mason said. Then he closed his eyes, imagined the light sabre at the top of its pendulum, and struck the ball.

"It went right through!" Cindy exclaimed.

"It's tough, but you could probably do it," Mason said.

"So, I guess that's a challenge," Cindy said as she placed her ball down and immediately swung her putter at it, effortlessly.

"Nice one," Mason said, impressed that her ball sailed through the danger.

Mason watched Cindy walk toward the hole and line her putt up. He noticed that she liked to talk and putt at the same time. Probably to relax her nerves, he thought.

She asked, "How'd you find out about this place?"

Mason waited for her to remove her ball from the hole and then shot his right into the back of the cup. "*Star Wars* is my all-time favourite movie. It's a classic." They began to walk toward the next hole, which had a big fibreglass replica of Han Solo duelling with a Storm Trooper. He continued, "I think I've watched *Star Wars, The Empire Strikes Back,* and *Return of the Jedi* at least twenty times each. So, when I heard they were opening a *Star Wars* mini-golf course, I flipped."

"I thought I was a big fan. But, you're a much bigger *Star Wars* nut than I'll ever be," Cindy said as she adjusted her long hair, which was flung back in a clip.

Mason felt much more relaxed around Cindy than he had expected to. He felt as though they really hit it off and he could just be himself around her. He didn't have to act cool or pretend to be Harrison Ford to click with her. It was just like they were hanging out, being friends. He was really enjoying it.

"What are you thinking?" Cindy asked as though she knew she was interrupting a deep thought.

Whoa, she's perceptive, Mason thought. "I was just working out the scores," he said. Then he paused to see if she bought it.

She did. "It's pretty obvious that you're winning, right?"

"Yeah, I'm ahead by two strokes," referring to the score card and doing a bit of quick math. "But it's not too late. You still have a chance."

"Thanks for not writing me out of the game."

Twenty minutes later, strolling off the eighteenth green, Cindy had reason to be confident. "That was one of the best comebacks I've ever seen," Mason complimented her.

"Did you let me win?"

"No, I swear."

He watched her just looking at him. Her hands were on her hips and her head was half tilted — it was obvious that she thought he was lying.

Mason pleaded his case, "I tried my best. Normally I beat everyone I play. But you're good." He didn't care if she thought that he let her win because boys were "supposed" to do that. There was no way he was going to pretend to lose, even to score points with a girl.

"I didn't want to tell you ... but before my parents split up my dad would take me to Meadow Brooks Country Club. That's where he plays golf. So, I've had a lot of practice."

"I knew there was a reason you're so good. You were just hustling me, keeping me in the lead, letting me think I'd win and then you caught me with my guard down," Mason said, putting the pieces together as though he were Sam Spade, Super Detective

"Pretty good, huh?" Cindy asked, proud of the win.

"Yeah, I'll have to remember that one." Mason continued toward the club house.

Cindy asked Mason, "Want to know why my parents split?"

Mason shrugged, not wanting to force her to tell him anything.

"It's okay. We're friends." Cindy continued, "I want you to know."

"Well, when you mentioned the split, I was a little curious," Mason said, being honest with her.

Cindy said, "My dad had a bit of a drinking problem. Actually he had a big drinking problem."

Mason was floored. He tried not to let it show, but it was tough.

"I'm not embarrassed or anything," Cindy said. "I like to tell people that are close to me."

"Is he okay now?" Mason asked.

"Yes, he's much much better," Cindy answered with a big smile. "He went into rehab and that helped him quit."

Mason was glad that Cindy felt close enough to tell him, but he wanted her to have a good time tonight. "How about a pop?" he offered.

"Sure. Loser pays?" Cindy asked.

"Funny," Mason quipped, really enjoying her sarcastic sense of humour.

After ordering two lemon-lime soft drinks, Mason heard Cindy say something that he thought she would have mentioned back on the first tee. "We lost the first game because the guys and girls refused to get along."

Mason took a big gulp of soda and said, "I know. If we lose our game next week then we definitely don't have a chance to go to the nationals in Ottawa."

"That's kind of why I wanted us to get together," Cindy said. "I have an idea. But I'm going to need your help. Big time."

Mason turned his attention from the galactic scenery of undiscovered planets, Jedi fighters, and Millennium Falcons orbiting the Death Star. He looked at Cindy and asked, "What are you thinking?"

A smile came across Cindy's face before she got the words out, foreshadowing her brilliant idea. "I think we should throw a party this weekend."

"A party," Mason repeated, realizing afterward how corny it must've sounded to repeat exactly what she had said.

"Yeah," Cindy continued. "We can all hang out and get to know one another outside the classroom, and even outside of basketball."

"I don't think Buckley and the guys will be interested in getting to know the girls," Mason answered honestly.

Cindy looked saddened by his lack of enthusiasm.

"But, it is worth a try," Mason immediately added. "You never know what will happen."

"Really? You think it may work?" Cindy asked, getting some of her enthusiasm back.

"For sure. At least you're coming up with ideas to save the team." Mason held out his right hand, feeling like a politician trying to bring together two factions of a divided country. "I'll do anything I can to help out."

"Excellent," Cindy said shaking his hand before polishing off the rest of her drink.

"The only problem is that I can't have a party at my place," Mason said. He was embarrassed that the apartment above the store was too cramped to have the entire team over.

"Don't worry. We can have it at my place." Cindy got up and crunched her white Styrofoam cup between her hands. She lined up her shot to the garbage container as though she were holding a basketball and tossed her drink into the bin.

"Two points!" Mason yelled out, imitating an NBA announcer. He did the same with his drink cup. Then he led Cindy out of the Intergalactic Park and Play, and they walked home in the crisp autumn air.

About two hundred yards from Cindy's house, probably a par three, Mason guestimated, he felt a sudden rush of confusion about his relationship with Cindy. For the first time that night, they hadn't talked in more than two minutes. What was she thinking about? Their relationship? Mason wondered. He didn't have the answer. Although he had the urge to hold her hand, he couldn't muster the courage to reach his hand out toward hers. What if she didn't respond, Mason anguished, what if she blasted him out of the sky like a B2 Bomber? He could just picture Cindy and her parents sitting Mason down in their living room, lecturing him on the dos and don'ts of appropriate dating etiquette. Mason would take notes so he wouldn't make a mistake on the next date ... if there would ever be a next date. Stop overreacting and just have fun, he ordered himself. But when they finally came to a stop at her front door, Mason had another big decision to make. THE FIRST KISS. Should he do it or not?

Cindy broke the long silence. "Thanks for a great time."

"I had a great time too," Mason said, wishing he had said it in a more creative way. "The party is going to be great. I'll try and talk the guys into coming when I see them tomorrow."

"Okay, that sounds perfect," Cindy said, sensing that their goodbye was becoming a bit uncomfortable.

Mason commanded himself to go for a quick kiss. But he knew that there was no way he was going to go for it. It just seemed too rushed, he thought. And if it felt that way then it obviously wasn't the right time. "Oh yeah, I almost forgot," Mason said, reaching into his blue jeans' pocket. He pulled out two packets of candy. "Have you ever tried this?"

"What is it?" Cindy asked.

"Super Sonic Pop Rock candy," Mason said, ripping the packets open and handing one to Cindy. "Try it."

She took the candy.

Mason dumped the entire thing into his mouth and indicated she should do the same.

"What does it do?" Cindy asked with a mouth full of tropical-flavoured nuggets.

"Give it a minute to kick in. My mom gets this from a place in New York. It's the best."

Just then the candy started to crackle in their mouths like kernels of corn bursting into popcorn.

"That's so cool. It feels like little explosions … it even sounds like little explosions!"

"I knew you'd like it," Mason said, glad that the pressure of the date was off and that they were just having fun again.

Walking away from Cindy's house, Mason could hear the loud crackle of the candy from both their mouths against the calm, crisp autumn night.

5

The Hustler

The school bell rang, and students poured out into the hallway from every room. Mason navigated toward his locker through the sea of grade-eight students.

Tyrone had to say "Hey, wait up" twice before Mason heard him.

"What's up?" Mason asked, deep in thought. He couldn't stop thinking about last night. He'd had such a great time.

"I called you last night and your mom said that you were out with a friend," Tyrone said, opening his locker.

Mason acted distracted, rummaging through his unkempt locker, pretending to look for anything that would buy him time to collect his thoughts. He couldn't let anyone know that he had gone out with Cindy, Mason told himself. Not even Tyrone could know that he had been hanging around with the so-called "enemy."

Tyrone broke Mason's train of thought by saying, "What are you looking for in there — Tutankhamen's treasures?"

"Where'd you learn that one?" Mason questioned.

"Mr. Brown's history class." Tyrone continued to be inspired by another in the series of *History of Civilization* lectures. "Tutankhamen was loaded. The guy was buried in treasures."

Mason slammed his locker shut, happy that he'd managed to direct Tyrone's questions away from his date with Cindy.

He walked with Tyrone through the crowded hall, asking him questions about Tutankhamen's life, continuing to distract Tyrone's attention away from the previous night. As Mason opened the school's old, blue doors and stepped into the cool autumn air, he asked Tyrone, "Do you think King Tutankhamen played basketball?"

Tyrone answered, "No. He couldn't have played b-ball because the sport was invented by a Canadian, James Naismith. But that's a whole other story in the history of the world."

Mason followed Tyrone around the side of the school to the basketball nets. He saw Buckley, Rodney, and the guys shooting buckets against the school's dilapidated net. They were all there, so Mason guessed he'd better find a way to hustle the guys into going to the party. He just had to find the right time.

Buckley yelled to Mason and Tyrone, "How about some Dead Man's one-on-one?"

"You're on," Mason answered. He loved to play Dead Man's one-on-one. It was a game the guys had made up to make one-on-one more interesting.

Rodney asked, "Are we talking the old version or the new one?"

Gavin piped in, "If the forward scores against the guard then that guard is a dead man and the next guy comes on to replace him."

"Yeah, but what happens if the guard steals the ball and makes a bucket?" Rodney asked the group, always a stickler for rules.

"Come on Rodney," Mason pleaded. "It's the same one we always play. If the guard nails a bucket then he moves to forward and someone else plays guard. The one with the most buckets as a forward wins."

"Oh, that's the old version," Rodney said, always pretending to know everything.

Mason unzipped his blue, sleeveless parka and tossed his knapsack on the ground against the side of the school's red-brick exterior. The parka was his favourite jacket to wear in the fall because he didn't get too hot in it. Although the afternoon was pretty cool and he could almost see his breath when he talked, Mason knew he would get hot as soon as he started to run around. As well, having no sleeves on his jacket made him more agile. His arms could move more freely, especially when he was deep in the zone.

"Game's on and I'm the first forward," Buckley announced as though he were king of the court.

Mason stood next to Gavin and watched Buckley take on Tyrone. Buckley started with a powerful drive to the net, trying to catch Tyrone off guard. But Mason knew that Tyrone was way too good to fall for that one. Tyrone proved Mason right when he stopped Buckley's dreams of scoring. Tyrone clipped the ball from Buckley, sending Buckley scrounging after the ball to regain control.

Gavin turned to Mason and said, "That was a good one. But now Buckley's mad."

Mason watched Buckley plough the ball past Tyrone. Using super-human strength, he forced the ball into the net.

"Who's next?" Buckley asked, overflowing with confidence.

"You're toast," Rodney claimed, replacing Tyrone.

Mason turned his attention away from the game to Gavin. "You think we have a chance of winning this year?"

Gavin answered, "We'll be lucky to win a single game."

"So what do you think we should do?" Mason asked, trying to get a better feeling for what the other guys were thinking.

"We have two choices," Gavin said, bending down to retie his shoelaces.

Even kneeling down, Gavin was the tallest guy on the team.

Gavin continued, "First choice is we transfer to a school with a better team."

Gavin laughed at his own joke. "What's the second choice, give up basketball and join the lacrosse team?" Mason said jokingly, getting a good laugh out of Gavin.

"The second choice is to find a way to play with the girls. But that's going to be impossible."

Mason turned back to the game, frustrated that practically everyone was extremely negative about playing with the girls. Going to Ottawa was looking more and more dismal, Mason thought. He half-heartedly watched Rodney try to beat Buckley off the court. But his mind kept racing with thoughts of having to ask the guys to go to Cindy's party. He though he would look like a real doorknob inviting the guys to a party. But deep down he truly believed that the team could play well if everyone could get along. He saw Buckley gain stride on a tired Rodney. That extra-stride advantage allowed Buckley to go for the net and bang in a two-pointer, wiping the floor with his opponent.

Buckley immediately turned to Mason and said, with the gleam of victory in his eyes, "You wanna go next, or should I play Isaac?"

Mason knew that Buckley was trying to humiliate Isaac in front of the other guys. "If you think you can handle it," Mason retorted, trying to knock Buckley down a peg.

"Let's rock." Buckley threw the ball to Mason, hard enough to let him know he meant business. "Take it to the baseline and give it to me when you're ready."

Mason watched Buckley take position at centre court. Instead of heading to the baseline, Mason held the ball in his hand and turned to the rest of the guys. "There's no way we're going to win this year." That got everyone's attention. "We probably won't even win a game."

"We're going all the way this year," Rodney blurted out in opposition.

"How?" Mason asked.

"By not passing to the girls," Rodney replied.

Mason saw Buckley go over to Rodney and high-five him.

Mason got serious, "You saw how we played in the first game. The other teams are too good. We need every player on the court working together if we're going to win."

"You worry too much," Buckley said. "Let's play."

"At least listen to what he has to say," Gavin butted in.

Here goes nothing, Mason thought as he said, "There's this party that we've all been invited to."

Isaac asked, "Whose party?"

"Cindy, Nikki, Anita, and the other girls are having a party."

This went over like a lead balloon with all the guys.

Mason continued, "If we don't try and get along with them then we're never going to go to Ottawa." Mason felt kind of selfish wanting to go to Ottawa so he could see Brent. But then he realized that deep down he wanted everyone to go to Ottawa so they could bring back the championship.

"There's no way I'm going to their little party," Buckley said.

"Guys, if we lose one more game then we're out of the running," Mason said, trying to convince them by appealing to their basketball sensibilities.

"I say we take a vote," Rodney said.

"Whatever you guys want," Mason added, trying not to sound too desperate. "Anybody who wants to go to Cindy's party, raise their hands."

No one raised his hand except for Mason and Isaac. But as soon as Buckley gave Isaac the evil eye, he quickly put his hand down.

"Looks like the party's out," Buckley said.

"Good," Rodney added. "It would be totally boring anyway." He started to snore, getting a chuckle out of the group.

There's no way that the guys would ever go to the party, Mason thought. Cindy was going to think he was a big loser for not being able to convince them.

Suddenly a brilliant idea hit him.

"Are you gonna just stand there?" Buckley asked Mason.

"How about a bet?" Mason blurted out to Buckley.

"I like bets," Buckley answered.

"What kind of bet?" Rodney asked.

"A slapshot competition. Whoever gets the most shots in, wins," Mason said.

"I'll bet you," Isaac said.

"But you already want to go to the party," Mason said.

"Oh yeah," Isaac muttered, realizing how silly he sounded.

"Are you in?" Mason asked Buckley.

"Slapshot competition? But we're playing basketball here," Buckley commented on the obvious.

Mason said, "We'll do it tomorrow when we go on our field trip to the Hockey Hall of Fame."

"Cool idea, Mason," Gavin said.

"Yeah, wicked idea," Tyrone added.

Isaac asked, "What are we betting?"

Mason said, "If I win then we all go to the party. If I lose then we don't go to the party."

"That's ridiculous," Rodney blurted out. "If Buckley wins then he has to get something better than just not going to the party."

"Fine ... then we'll have a party at my place," Mason added, thinking quickly on his feet.

Buckley said, "We have a party at your place and you have to be my in-school butler for a week."

"No way," Mason said.

"Then the deal's off," Buckley replied.

What should he do? He was in a pretty desperate situation, he admitted to himself. "You're on. But, I'll only be your butler for a day," Mason said, trying to salvage some self-respect.

"We have a deal," Buckley confirmed. "Now let's finish this Dead Man."

"You're a brave man," Tyrone said to Mason. Mason entered the court and walked toward the baseline questioning whether or not he had done the right thing. The stakes were very high and he had to be cool, he realized.

"Give me the ball," Buckley demanded.

Mason dribbled the ball a few times and then threw it to Buckley, starting the game. Buckley came at him like a freight train barrelling across country. Mason stopped him by hooking the ball out of his hands. As Mason waited for Buckley to retrieve the ball, yellow and orange leaves rustled on the asphalt, fanned by the approaching arctic air. During Buckley's next assault, Mason managed to gain possession of the ball again. He dribbled it out to centre court and decided on the best way to get past Buckley. Mason edged forward and slowly made his way as far left as possible. Then with a big huff of energy, he drove toward the net in an arc pattern, hoping to intercept with the hoop at just the right time.

Mason saw that Buckley wasn't able to stay within elbow distance of his arc. So he kicked in his after-burners and pushed even harder toward the net. His scopes targeted the hoop as he expertly switched mid-dribble from using his right hand to using his left hand. There's no way he can stop me now, Mason thought.

The instant before Mason was about to release the ball into the air he realized that there were bigger things at stake than this little one-on-one game. He knew that if he missed the bucket and let Buckley win, it would give Buckley false confidence. Just as Cindy had let Mason keep his lead in miniature golf until the very end. With both feet in the air, Mason put a bit of extra spin on the ball, sending it off the backboard and back into play. Mason watched as Buckley snatched the ball and made the easy two-pointer.

"I win," Buckley announced.

Mason knew that he had made the right move. Because tomorrow's match at the Hockey Hall of Fame was much more important than a game of Dead Man.

"You're next, Isaac," Buckley said.

Isaac replace Mason on the court. Mason ran to the side entrance of the school and popped in to get a slurp of water. When he got to the water fountain he saw Cindy. Before drinking he said to her excitedly, "Guess what? The party's on."

6

Risky Business

Mason watched from the back seat as the prehistoric yellow school bus shot a chimney full of black smoke into the atmosphere. The bus turned left onto Parliament Street and headed south toward Front Street and the Hockey Hall of Fame. Mason thought that it was strange being out in the real world in the middle of the afternoon. Usually he'd be in class looking out the window and wondering what was going on out there. Mason studied the midday traffic ... people rushing to meetings, blue sedans cutting off beige jeeps just to get to that important meeting ten seconds earlier. Mason found the action outside boring and turned his attention back to the festivities inside the school bus. The yellow monster was a hive of activity as students kibitzed about everything and anything. Mason was sitting on the aisle next to Rodney.

Buckley was across the aisle from Mason and as he adjusted the beak of his bright-red Nike baseball cap, he said, "Hey Mason, you catch the basketball game on TV last night?"

"No, I missed it," Mason replied.

"I thought you were like the biggest fan?"

"Yeah, but I was busy," Mason said, not wanting to tell the guys that he had had to help his Mom unload a big box of toothbrushes in their convenience store. It took forever to hang all those toothbrushes on the long thin racks. Mason had organized them all by colour and size.

"Well, Toronto wiped out the competition — just like I'm going to do to you," Buckley said smugly.

Mason decided to let Buckley's comments slide and keep him thinking he was the best at everything.

"What's the point of having this hockey competition anyway?" Isaac asked from behind his brick-thick tortoiseshell glasses.

"It's to see if we have to go to Mason's little party," Buckley answered.

"Don't you guys get it — we can't play with half a team!" Mason said, tired of the guys not understanding the importance of playing with the girls.

Everyone was taken aback by Mason's anger.

"So why don't you go sit with the girls?" Buckley asked sarcastically.

He should go sit with them, maybe take a seat between Cindy and Anita, Mason thought. But instead, he swallowed his exasperation, waiting to let it out during his slapshot showdown with Buckley.

* * * * *

The Hockey Hall of Fame, in the heart of downtown Toronto, was one of the coolest places Mason had ever visited. It was like a museum of hockey. Mason was awestruck as he wandered around. "I wish we could look around ourselves," he said to Tyrone and Gavin.

Gavin asked, "Why do we have walk around in a line?"

"Because they think we're kids," Tyrone answered.

"Oh yeah, I bet I know more about hockey trivia than anyone who works here," Gavin boasted.

"Check this out," Mason said, pointing to the entrance of the Montreal Canadiens' dressing room. He darted in a bit ahead of the group to see the mock-up. "It's just like being transported into the real dressing room," Mason said to Tyrone, who had caught up to him.

"This is so cool!" Tyrone agreed. "This is going to be my spot when I make the NHL," Tyrone continued, picking out a locker for himself.

Mason checked out the different lockers on display, while the rest of the class poured into the dressing room. Everything looked authentic to Mason as he inspected every detail of a locker — from the jerseys to the helmets.

"Over here," Mason heard Gavin say. Mason followed him out of the Canadiens' hang-out and into the Toronto Maple Leafs' dressing room. Mason was speechless. It was like he was standing in the real thing! It was identical to the way he remembered it when he toured Maple Leaf Gardens with Brent. Mason looked toward the exit of the locker room trying to picture it leading to the pathway that takes the players to the ice. This is exactly what it must feel like for the players before they play a big game, Mason imagined.

"You ready, hotshot?" Buckley barked from behind Mason.

Buckley shattered Mason's hockey daydream and yanked him back to reality. He turned to see that Buckley, the Nike-man himself, was full of confidence. Mason didn't have to answer Buckley — they both knew that it was time to play.

Without any of the teachers or students noticing, Mason followed Buckley out of the Toronto Maple Leafs' dressing room toward the wrist-shot exhibit. It was early afternoon at the Hockey Hall of Fame so there wasn't a huge weekend-size crowd or line-up.

"The teacher's going to give us a month's detention if we get caught," Mason warned Buckley.

"What's your point?" Buckley answered, the words *caught* or *danger* not even in his vocabulary.

They reached the exhibit just as an elderly couple finished playing on it. The exhibit consisted of a Plexiglas goalie attached to an NHL-size hockey net. Mason noticed that the only openings for the puck to enter through were in each of the four corners. A stand full of cardboard fans surrounded the net. The cardboard people looked on, but Mason got an eerie feeling that they were supporting Buckley instead of him. It was like being in an arena full of frozen scarecrows.

"I'll go first," Buckley claimed as he grabbed a hockey stick and placed it in front of the black puck. "Whichever hole I put the puck in, you have to get it in the same one. First one to three wins."

Mason listened to Buckley make up the rules as he went. It was like taking a shot from the blue line, Mason calculated. Buckley lined a shot up and then flicked it into the lower-left corner. It was Mason's turn. He took the stick from Buckley and aimed his shot at the same corner. Just concentrate, Mason told himself, trying to ignore the cardboard people. Whack! He slammed a perfect line drive into the opening.

"Give me that stick," Buckley ordered, getting right down to business. The next shot whizzed off a bit of the goalie and penetrated the top-right corner.

Mason immediately took his shot, not letting the pressure of going second get to him. Relieved, he watched the puck sail into the same opening as Buckley had scored on. He looked up to see Rodney, Isaac, Gavin, and Tyrone watching. "I didn't even notice you guys," Mason said.

Gavin answered, "We didn't want to distract you."

Buckley directed his last shot at the bottom-right hole, but it recoiled off the goal post.

This was it, Mason thought. If he got it in he would win. "Because you missed I can go for any hole I want."

"No way. You can't make up the rules as you go," Buckley said, knowing full well that it was he who had made up the rules on the fly.

"Whatever," Mason said, not wanting to argue with the guy. He brought his blade down on the puck and tried to slapshot it into the bottom right corner. His heart sank as the puck zoomed way off target.

"We're going into overtime," Buckley said. "Next one to nail a shot wins."

Mason realized that his mind was in basketball mode. He had to think back to the summer when he played roller hockey for the Cabbagetown Blues. Then it hit him. He prayed that Buckley would go for one of the top corners because Mason's wrist shot was his strongest shot.

"Get it in," Rodney cheered Buckley.

Buckley took aim and whacked the puck at the net.

He went for the upper corner. Mason watched the puck take flight and head toward the opening. It missed by a hair and bounced back. It's as though the Plexiglas goalie made the big save! Mason joked to himself.

Just then, Mr. Brown walked up to the exhibit with the entire class. "What's going on here?"

"We got lost so we thought we'd just wait here for you," Buckley lied.

Mr. Brown processed the information and then nodded, accepting Buckley's story. "Fine. Take your shot so the rest of us can play."

"Go ahead," Buckley said to Mason, visibly enjoying the fact that everyone was watching.

Mason stood in the centre of the exhibit and looked around at the class watching him. He saw the cardboard fans staring down at him, just waiting to laugh and boo when he missed the shot. Stay cool, Mason told himself. It was just like playing roller hockey. He scanned the rows of cardboard people and then looked around at the class and noticed Cindy. She didn't even know that this shot would determine whether or not they had the party. Mason thought it was ironic that he was in the middle of a hockey shootout to keep his basketball team together. He walked up to the puck, stared at the opening in the top-right corner of the net. It was just like his dad had taught him to do, Mason thought. The number one rule was to keep his eyes on net, rather than on the puck. It was weird — Mason could remember the exact day that his dad had told him that. Mason actually felt his father's presence, although he knew full well that that was physically impossible. He wished his dad was alive to root him on.

"Shoot it," Buckley yelled.

Mason took aim at the puck's final destination, visualized the puck going into the net, and executed his patented wrist shot.

Everyone watched the puck sail through the air and pass directly through the opening.

"I did it!" Mason yelled out to Buckley.

Buckley said, "You got lucky," and walked off.

Most of the class applauded loudly, not realizing that this had been a very serious match. It looked as if he wouldn't have to be Buckley's butler, Mason thought. Then he spotted Cindy in the crowd, and they exchanged smiles. The best part was, the party was on.

7

Like It's 1999

The party was shaping up to be anything but a smashing hit. Mason sat quietly on an extra-wide, lime-green leather couch in Cindy's living room. All the girls sat, scattered around him on other pieces of ultra-hip furniture. Nikki and Anita were the last of the girls to show up. Since then they had all just sat there staring into the fancy grey, plastered ceiling. It was like a topographical map — with jutting peaks, abated valleys, and really interesting geographical patterns.

That would make a really cool planet, Mason thought, staring at the ceiling while trying to suppress his feeling of impending doom regarding the party.

"You like?" Cindy asked.

"Yeah, it's really neat. I've never seen a ceiling like this before," Nikki said, the back of her cropped blond hair fanning out as she leaned in against a royal-blue chair. "Who did it?"

"My mom is an artist and she does all kinds of cool work," Cindy explained. "What do you think, Mason?"

"Huh?" Mason said, not really listening to their conversation. He was too busy worrying about the party. If the guys broke their promise and didn't show up, he figured there really wouldn't be much of a chance for the team. Anyway, Mason had won the shootout fair and square. If Buckley didn't show he should be Mason's slave for a week. Besides all that, Mason had helped Cindy and her mom set up for the party all day. If the guys didn't make it, all that work would be for nothing. "Oh, yeah. I like the ceiling a lot." Mason looked around the living room, proof of his decorating efforts. It was decked out with streamers, posters of NBA basketball players, and crazy glow-in-the-dark sketches of hoops with balls going through them.

"You like the decorations?" Mason asked the girls.

They studied the room. They had been staring at the ceiling for so long that they hadn't noticed their other surroundings. Anita and Nikki started to giggle.

"Yeah, it's cool," Nikki said. She was checking out a life-sized poster of Dennis Rodman. "Totally cool hair."

"You should see the backyard," Cindy said. "Mason and my mom spent most of the day setting it up."

Mason smirked. The way he figured it, he would do almost anything to make this party work. Even waste his precious Saturday laying down lights and streamers in Cindy's house and backyard.

"Later, if things pick up, my big brother's band will play for us," Cindy said. "They played at the high school battle of the bands and came in second."

"What kind of music do they play?" Anita asked.

"Mostly a grunge-reggae mix," she said, with the kind of pride only a member of the family tree could possess.

"Grunge and reggae mix?" Nikki questioned. "I've never heard of that before."

"It's their own style. It's experimental."

Suddenly the doorbell rang. Mason sprang from his spot on the couch and zipped to the front door. He opened it up and there were the guys.

"Well are you going to let us in, or just stand there?" Buckley asked.

"Sure," Mason said, stepping aside so the gang could trample in. "Hey, Tyrone," Mason said. "What took you guys so long?"

The rest of the guys headed into the living room as Mason and Tyrone spoke in the hallway.

"They were just a little hesitant," Tyrone answered. "But they realize that the good of the team depends on getting along with the girls. So here we are."

"Thanks for pushing them."

When Mason and Tyrone ambled into the living room a second later, they found the boys and the girls sitting on opposite sides of the rug. This was going to be a very long party, Mason thought. There had to be something he could do. But Cindy beat him to it.

"Hey, who wants to go to the backyard and shoot hoops?" she asked.

Without hesitation everyone jumped up and the party was underway.

* * * * *

Mason watched Gavin and Nikki playing one-on-one using Cindy's bright-orange, garage-mounted hoop. Cindy said her dad had put it up when she first got interested in the sport several years earlier. She told Mason that there was a time when she was so hooked on the game, she would spend all day and all evening out in front of the garage shooting hoops by herself. Her dad used to say that she liked basketball as much as he liked golf. Cindy had explained to Mason that she thought if she put in enough effort she could be the first woman in the NBA. She had told him that one summer her ball actually went flat from overuse.

Gavin took a shot and missed. Nikki rushed in and ... two points. She passed back to Gavin and he immediately popped a shot into the air ... nothing but net ... two points.

Mason watched on, excited that guys and girls were finally interacting.

"So who do you think will be the NBA's highest scorer this year?" Nikki asked Gavin.

"I figure Jordan will take it," he said. "He's got supernatural powers or something."

"Yeah, totally. He's a superhuman."

"I think he's got wings," Gavin said.

That got a bit of a laugh out of the girls.

"Even if Jordan doesn't win you can bet that someone else on the Bulls will." Nikki took a shot. "Maybe Pippin."

"I actually like the Shaq."

"The Shaq's good but he can't carry the team the way Jordan can," Nikki retorted.

Mason was happy with the way things were going on the backyard court. As he strolled over to the refreshment table he thought that if everyone started talking the way Nikki and Gavin were, the team just might work.

Mason looked over to the back door of the house to see Cindy walk outside with a tray of party sandwiches. The bright-metallic tray supported a stack of them. Mason was trying to decide whether he preferred a salmon, tuna, or a chicken sandwich. On the other hand, he loved the way peanut butter pinwheels looked with the banana rolled up in the middle. But the best thing about party sandwiches was that you could try all different kinds without getting totally stuffed.

Cindy placed the tray on the table. "Mason do you want to bring out your bowl of punch?"

"Sure," Mason answered. But he didn't, really. Well, at least not until he could have a sandwich or two.

Earlier that day, Mason had brought over bottles of pop from his mom's store. He brought ginger ale, cola, root beer, and orange juice. Then he mixed them all together in a big, glass bowl. When the mixture was all blended up he added his secret ingredient — a drop of grenadine. He thought it was the coolist punch in the world. He called it Mason's Special Brew. If no one else wanted any, he could probably chug down the whole bowl himself.

Mason walked outside with the big punch bowl, feeling like a waiter on a sail boat and trying not to spill a drop. As he traipsed across the patio he couldn't believe how heavy and awkward the big, glass dish was.

"What's in the punch?" Buckley asked as he walked across the porch to Mason.

"A bunch of things," Mason responded as he placed the bowl on a bizzare, shiny picnic table.

"Well, I bet I brought a better drink than that."

Mason didn't like the boastful tone of Buckley's voice. He hated it when Buckley went on like he was the best. It was bad enough that he always had new shoes, new sweatpants, and new shirts. But when he started to get boastful, Mason couldn't handle being in the same city as him. It made Mason feel about two centimetres tall.

"So what did you bring?" Mason asked.

Rodney started to laugh.

"I can't show you now," he said nodding his head toward Cindy's mom, who was standing over at the far end of the patio. "When she goes I'll show you." Buckley went toward the garage basketball net where Gavin and Nikki were still playing one-on-one. Then Mason saw him disappear with Rodney behind a big wooden gate that adjoined the house to the garage.

"Buckley's full of it," Mason uttered to himself. But his curiosity was piqued.

"How's the party going, Mason?" Cindy's mom asked as she poured herself a double glass of punch.

"Really well," he replied. "Everybody's talking. People are even playing basketball over at the garage."

"I'm glad."

"Yeah, I think we really have a chance now that everybody is willing to work together." Mason picked up a few party sandwiches. He gulped down a tuna triangle and savoured every morsel.

"That's great to hear," she said.

Mason wanted to tell her that it was really cool of her to let them have the party at her house but his mouth was so crammed he just nodded.

"Keep having fun." She walked inside.

Mason checked out the yard. The streamers that he had hung between the big maple trees were still where he had put them. But most important, he saw all his friends talking. Isaac and Anita were sitting on lawn chairs chatting. Probably quizzing each other on basketball trivia at which they were both expert. Cindy and Tyrone were over by the weird picnic bench Cindy's mom had made. It was a perfect night, Mason thought, just like the night of the mini-golf date with Cindy.

Then he wondered where Buckley and Rodney had gone.

Now that Cindy's mom was inside he was clear to go look for them. He went over to the court where Nikki and Gavin were now on their fifth game of one-on-one ... it was anyone's game. After a word with them he went over to the wooden fence he had seen Buckley and Rodney go through earlier.

He opened it and saw the guys standing in the shadow of the house, looking suspicious.

"What's going on, guys?"

"Hey, Ashbury," Buckley said. "Come to be a real man, hey?"

At this point Mason could see that Buckley was hiding something in his new Nike bomber jacket. But he couldn't tell what it was. "What are you talking about, Buckley?" Mason asked.

Buckley looked him right in the eye like they were having a stand-off on a dirt street in a small town in the Wild West. Then he pulled out a bottle of beer. "I'm talking about this," he said as he handed Mason the bottle. "Go on, have some."

"I don't know. It's not really cool to drink at someone else's place," Mason said, trying not to appear to be too much of a wimp. Besides, he thought it sounded like a good excuse. Thinking about the beer reminded him of the times he had spent watching *Hockey Night in Canada* with his dad. Mason was always allowed a sip of his dad's beer. It had been tradition.

"What are you, chicken?" Rodney asked as he took the bottle and had a big swig.

"No. I've had beer before, I just don't think Cindy would like it if we drank here." He wasn't lying. He knew from Cindy talking about her dad how much drinking bothered her.

"You've never had beer before. I know you're lying," Buckley announced, gulping down a bubbly mouthful.

Mason was starting to get angry with them. He hated being called a liar and he hated it even more that they weren't respecting Cindy's house.

"Bock bock bock bock ..." They started to flap their arms.

"Isn't the chicken thing kind of prehistoric?" Mason asked, trying to make them feel stupid.

"Aren't you kind of a mama's boy?" Buckley barked, taunting Mason with the long-necked bottle.

"Fine," Mason said as he grabbed the dark-brown bottle. "I'll have some, if it will shut you up." Mason wrapped his lips around the bottle and slowly started to drink. He let the cool beer slide down his throat. He actually enjoyed the exotic taste. It was just as he had remembered from years earlier. Suddenly, he was bombarded with a flood of memories of his dad, images of the two of them watching Stanley Cup playoffs.

Just then the wooden gate swung open.

"Mason," Cindy said in a sharp voice. "What are you doing?"

He flinched and the bottle fell to the grass ... beer drained into the soil.

"Get out. Get out of here!" Cindy had begun to shout.

"But ..." Mason tried to get a word in and explain what he had done. But Cindy's yelling just drowned him out.

"I never want to talk to you again. Get out of here!" She slammed the wooden fence shut and left Mason standing there, cold and stunned. The harsh reality of what he had done crashed down on him. What was he thinking?

8

Hang Over

Mason pounded Isaac's official NBA-issue basketball into the Riverdale Park basketball court so hard that anyone watching would swear he was denting the pavement. He moved down court, deked out Tyrone and performed a flawless layup.

"Another two," Mason yelled as he tossed the ball over to Gavin and retreated up court. The sun was unusually warm for a fall day. The leaves had mostly disappeared and the park's scenery seemed bare and vacant without its summer vegetation.

Gavin started to dribble the b-ball. After a beat he made a bounce pass over to Tyrone who drove it up court. Tyrone faked out Isaac and moved further up court toward Mason, who was now in guard mode. Gavin streaked up court parallel to his wing-man, Tyrone. At just the right moment he performed his best Big Country Reeves by cuing Tyrone for the pass. Tyrone flung the ball skyward. Just as the twirling ball was about to reach Gavin ... interception. Mason picked it out of the air with such velocity and force it was as though the ball was frozen in time. Then he flew down court at warp speed and slammed the ball home.

"Wow, way to take it downtown!" Tyrone said to Mason. "Your game's on fire."

Mason didn't respond. He was brooding, staring at the dying weeds that had once flourished between the cracks in the court's cement. He was sorting out his feelings and he wasn't at the point where he could talk about anything.

"Yeah," Gavin added. "You've really got the golden touch today."

Isaac piped in, "Now that we're friends with the girls we'll all play together. And I bet we'll even have a shot at going to Ottawa."

"Totally," Tyrone said.

"I don't know," Mason said in a low, depressed voice. His mind was on Cindy. That bottle of beer was like a photograph etched into his brain.

"Mason, we're going to kick in our next game," Gavin said, trying to convince him.

"Especially if you keep playing like that," Isaac added.

"Guys, the North York Jazz are the best team in the league. There is practically no way we'll take them," Mason said, still staring at the grey cement. "I hear they have a centre who's over six feet tall."

"That giant thing is a myth," Gavin said.

"Either way, they've been the city champs four years running. They'll be really tough to beat," Mason reinforced. "Our team lost big time last year and we were all guys."

"But if we try hard enough and we work together we might be able to beat them. Then we can go to Ottawa," Isaac said, as upbeat as a cheerleader.

"I don't know," Mason said. He really wanted to go to Ottawa but he was feeling pessimistic. Worse, the thought that he had upset Cindy plagued him.

Tyrone started to bounce the ball to indicate he wanted to keep the four-man game going instead of talking. "Come on, let's play. Enough of the depressing talk."

Hang Over

Mason started to walk back up to his defensive position. Tryone and Gavin were now passing back and forth.

"We definitely have a chance. That's all I'm saying," Isaac reiterated to Mason.

As the scrimmage continued, Mason thought about how he just couldn't share their optimism. Cindy wasn't talking to him and that meant that he was hurting. So much so that he was hogging the ball and playing ten times more aggressively than usual. He knew that when playing with only three other guys he could act like this. But if he brought the same kind of untamed attitude to a league game the coach would bench him in a millisecond. Underneath it all he blamed Buckley. It was Buckley who had pressured him into drinking the beer. "I'm glad Buckley's not here," Mason blurted out.

There was silence from the other guys, who were busy jockeying for position near the net.

If Buckley had shown up at the Sunday scrimmage game, as he usually did, Mason wasn't sure what he would have done. He might even have punched him and gotten into a scrap.

Other than the occasional mix-up he got into during hockey, Mason had only ever been in one fight. It was with a guy from the neighbourhood named Jimmy Camby. Everyone called him Cam. One Saturday afternoon Cam came into the convenience store while Mason was working. Mason was busy cleaning a shelf full of leaking tomato sauce when he saw Cam steal several items from the store's big green plastic toy bin. When Mason confronted him, Cam ran like the wind. The whole incident happened around the time when Mason's mom was having financial trouble, and Mason knew that every little trinket counted. So he raced out of the store after Cam. About a block and a half away, he confronted him.

"Give me back what you stole," Mason said.

"I don't know what you're talking about, Ashbury," Cam said.

"The squirt gun and water rocket in your right jacket pocket."

"If you want it, you'll have to take it from me," Cam challenged, thinking he scared Mason just because he was bigger. But Mason wasn't scared, and he lunged at Cam, fists flailing.

In the end, Mason seized back the stolen goods and, in return, left Cam with a black eye. But Mason knew that getting in a fight wasn't smart. There was one major reason for this: Greg, Cam's larger and older brother. When Greg heard that Mason had beaten up Cam, he went after him. Just before Greg was about to make Mason eat his ten speed, Mason's mom intervened and settled the issue. She made Mason apologize for fighting. At the same time, Mrs. Camby found out what her son was up to and made him pay for what he had taken. She also made him apologize to Mason. After the incident, Mason and Cam were actually friends for a term. They hung out until grade school was over. In the end, the friendship disintegrated when they went to different schools.

Back at the scrimmage, Tyrone had possession in his zone. He whipped a pass to Gavin who flung it back just as quickly. Then Tyrone burst past Isaac, pushed his knees skyward and tipped one in.

"That's two," Tyrone hollered, happy the give-and-go had gone so flawlessly.

Mason watched with a feeling of utter helplessness. He was no longer playing aggressively. He was too distracted by the beer incident to help Isaac out. If he didn't get over this thing soon he was going to be of no use to the Raptors. They would have to bring down the six-foot Jazz giant without him. The more he thought about the incident and all the trouble the fight had caused, the more he realized that he wasn't truly that mad at Buckley. Buckley might have offered him the beer but Mason didn't have to bow to the pressure and drink it.

Mason knew he was more mad at himself than anyone. And his game was going to suck unless he snapped out of it. He started to get angry again.

Isaac had the ball and was doing the offensive shuffle as best he could. He was actually doing an okay job keeping the ball away from Tyrone and Gavin. As he wound up to take one of his patented three-pointers, Mason jetted in out of nowhere and grabbed the ball from his teammate. Mason took it downtown, aimed, shot, and missed.

"That's it," Isaac yelled. "I've got to go home. My mom and dad are taking me out for an early dinner at my grandparents." He picked up his basketball and clutched it between his arm and body.

Mason knew that Isaac was lying. Issac just didn't want to play with him anymore.

"All right, I guess we'll see each other tomorrow," Gavin said.

"See ya," Mason muttered, hanging his head.

The ritual Sunday scrimmage was over for another week. Isaac walked off with his ball, Gavin headed home, and Mason and Tyrone turned to walk toward their homes. They made their way along the park's gravel trail, which was enclosed by big, barren trees and dead shrubs. Eventually they reached the comfort of the cement sidewalk of Atlantic Avenue.

"What's wrong with you today?" Tyrone asked.

"Nothing," Mason responded.

"Come on, man. You weren't playing like you and you're definitely not acting like you." Tyrone started to kick a small rock that was lying on the sidewalk. He soccer-kicked it and Mason received the pass.

"I don't know, Tyrone. I think it was the party yesterday."

"The party was great. We totally got along with all the girls and I know that'll make us a stronger team."

"Yeah, I'm glad everyone got along. But my problem is bigger." Mason was still kicking the rock and sent a quick shot over to his friend who continued with it down the sidewalk. "I really upset someone."

"Who?" Tyrone asked, stopping in his tracks.

"Forget it." Mason continued to walk and Tyrone caught up.

"No way. If you're upset we gotta talk." Tyrone continued the rock soccer. "That's what being buddies is all about."

"I guess," Mason said, feeling glum.

"So?"

"It's Cindy. I upset her."

"Ooh, Cindy," Tyrone said in the same sarcastic tone grade-five boys use when harassing each other about girls. "You like her."

Mason didn't respond. He just gave Tyrone a "grow up" look.

"Sorry," Tyrone said. "I was just razzing you. So, what happened?" Tyrone passed the rock back to Mason. "You guys looked like you were getting along great." Mason flicked it up to a crosswalk then stopped to wait for a bright orange Volkswagen bug to pass them.

"Tangerine dream," Mason said.

"Huh?" Tyrone had no idea what he was talking about.

"The orange car. Brent's dad used to have one exactly like that. He called it the Tangerine Dream." Mason said as the Volkswagen putted past them. When the street was clear, Mason booted the rock so it landed in the middle of the crosswalk. Then he went after it.

"So, Cindy?" Tyrone asked trying to get back to Mason's problem.

"Yeah, I really upset her. I don't know if she'll ever talk to me again."

"What happened?"

"It was at the party. Everyone was off doing their own thing and having fun when Buckley came up to me and said he had something to show me. So I went over to where he was hiding and he pulled out a beer."

"He was drinking?" Tyrone asked, surprised.

"Well, the point was that I was drinking too and Cindy caught us." Mason didn't want to mention the stuff about Cindy's dad because Cindy had said she told only those who were close to her. He kicked the rock up the other side of the curb and Tyrone went after it.

"Why don't you just apologize to her?" Tyrone asked.

It sounded logical enough, Mason thought. But there were circumstances, like Cindy's dad, that messed up the simple solution. "I just don't think I can."

"Sure you can," Tyrone said as he kicked the rock into a telephone pole and Mason grabbed the rebound. "It just takes guts to admit that you did something wrong."

"Sure," Mason agreed. Tyrone was saying things Mason already knew. In most situations Mason would have had no difficulty apologizing. But for a multitude of reasons this was different than any other messed-up situation he had been in.

"Just yesterday I had to apologize to my mom for smashing her favourite vase," Tyrone said.

"But that was an accident," Mason said. "I didn't do this by accident. I actually thought about it before I drank." As Mason flicked the rock through his legs and over to Tyrone he started to feel even more depressed.

"It might feel like an impossible situation but I bet you'll get through it," Tyrone mused.

"You sound like my mom."

"My mom actually said that to me last week when I thought I'd failed my math test," Tyrone explained.

Mason and Tyrone kicked the rock back and forth a few more times. Then Tyrone had to turn down Cartier Street where he lived. Mason continued to think about his problems. He knew that Tyrone meant well in offering his advice. But he wasn't helping. He just didn't understand the situation.

Even if Mason did apologize to Cindy, he doubted she'd forgive him. To top it off, he knew he wouldn't be any good to the Raptors in his condition. They needed everyone on the team to be in peak shape to have a shot at beating the Jazz. Walking along the barren Cabbagetown street Mason came to the conclusion that everything was bleak and that there wasn't a chance of the team going to the Ottawa nationals, or of him seeing Brent.

9

Mission Impossible

It was minutes before the start of the big game against the Jazz. Mason popped out of the Cabbagetown Raptors' locker room expecting to see a hoard of paparazzi and fans eager for the big photo opportunity. Maybe one day when he was in the big league, Mason thought. He liked to walk alone along the narrow stretch of corridor between the locker room and the gymnasium. It was amazing to see all the photos on the wall, he thought as he checked out some of the old black-and-white pictures of championship teams past.

"Hey Mason, wait up," Tyrone yelled.

Mason heard the echo of Tyrone's voice bounce back and forth between the narrow antique walls.

Tyrone asked, "What are you looking at?"

"Just thinking about stuff," Mason answered. He turned his gaze away from the old pictures, leaving the young champions to do what they always did ... hang on the wall.

Mason and Tyrone reached the end of the corridor and pushed open the heavy double doors leading into the big gym. Standing at the base of the bleachers waiting for Mason were Patricia and Jim.

Mason turned to Tyrone, "I'll catch you in a bit."

"No problem," Tyrone answered. "And Mason, don't worry about Cindy ... things'll work out."

Mason approached Patricia and Jim as Tyrone trotted off.

"Hi, honey!" Patricia said. "You look so cute in your uniform."

"Mom," Mason said, in a tone to let her know to stop embarrassing him.

Jim cut in. "So, little buddy, ready for the big game?"

Mason replied with a not so convincing "Yeah, I'm ready." But the truth was that he felt nervous. He was anxious about making it to the finals in Ottawa and jittery about seeing Cindy.

"Jim and I are really proud of you, Mason," Patricia said. "We'll be in the eighth row, rooting you on."

Just then, Mason saw Cindy head in with Anita.

"Oh, look," Patricia announced, "there's Cindy. Let's say hi."

"She's busy," Mason interrupted. Mason looked over to Cindy, made eye contact and then turned away.

"Is everything okay?" Patricia asked.

Moms can pick up on everything, like doppler radar, Mason concluded. "Everything's fine, Mom. The game's about to start … we'll talk later." Mason began to move toward the Raptor's bench.

"Good luck," Patricia and Jim said simultaneously before taking their seats in the packed gymnasium.

* * * * *

Game action began when the black-and-white jerseyed referee raised the basketball into the air precisely between Mason and the Jazz centre. The game clock started to count down and all eyes in the gym followed the round leather ball. Mason swiped his right paw in the path of the basketball and made contact with it as it arced downward through the air. He directed the sphere toward Nikki, who was playing left forward.

"Set up the play," Mason said as he watched Nikki take control. She began to get pressure from a Jazz forward who covered her like paint on a wall.

"Bring it back," Tyrone said.

Nikki gave the ball a low bounce and then tossed it with one hand to Tyrone who was covering the back court.

Mason clapped and yelled, "Way to go." He knew that Nikki was a very capable player because she didn't give into the offensive pressure by aimlessly tossing the ball into enemy territory. Instead she made the smart play by sending it to a guard so they could regroup.

"Get in the clear," Tyrone belted as he dribbled the ball aggressively.

Mason pointed toward Gavin who had cleared himself a stretch of open space.

Tyrone saw Mason point and made the quick pass to Gavin.

Gavin brought the ball past the three-point line and passed it into the zone.

Mason got to the ball's arrival point and tossed it against the backboard. The ball bounced up off the rim and down into Nikki's hands. Mason watched Nikki rabbit-jump into the air and nail the two-pointer. Mason high-fived her, not understanding how he could have missed such a rudimentary shot.

"Stop the celebration," Coach Pollinoffsky ordered from the sideline. "Play defence."

Mason sprinted backward, determined to get his game in shape. The sooner I score my first bucket, Mason thought, the sooner I'll be in the game. But what bothered him deep down was that he couldn't get his mind off Cindy. How could he have been so stupid at the party, he thought for the hundredth time.

"Watch out!" Isaac yelled.

Mason realized that he was so deep in thought that he had run backwards along the length of the court and had just about tripped over Isaac.

"I'm the one who trips over people," Isaac joked. "I thought you had eyes in the back of your head."

Mason said, "Sorry, man," but offered no excuse because he knew none was justified.

The Jazz scored a bucket to tie up the game, and the two teams fell into a routine — the Raptors scored, then the Jazz scored ... tit-for-tat.

During a shift on the bench, Mason watched his team play a pretty good game.

"You okay?" Gavin asked while dumping a gallon of water from the water bottle over his head.

"Just a little sluggish tonight, but I'll turn around," Mason answered in the highest spirit he could possibly summon.

Gavin hit with, "Yeah, but you've only scored four points all quarter."

"Thanks for reminding me," Mason said with a hint of sarcasm in his voice.

On his other side, Tyrone leaned in close to Mason, "Is it the girl?"

Mason knew the exact girl Tyrone was talking about ... but playing badly had nothing to do with Cindy. "No," Mason answered, stone-faced.

Tyrone said, "There's nothing wrong with admitting it. If you do, then at least you can do something about it."

"Like what am I supposed to do?" Mason shrugged.

"I don't know, I'm not the relationship expert," Tyrone shrugged back.

Gavin said, "I guess you could talk to her."

Mason looked at Gavin like he had ten heads. "Just talk to her? You guys don't understand."

The coach turned his attention from the court-side action to the bench. "Mason, Buckley, and Anita." Their heads turned toward the coach simultaneously, as if it had been choreographed in a big Hollywood blockbuster. The Mighty Raptors — Part Deux, Mason joked to himself. Then he headed back on the court to replace Cindy in the centre position. Usually the players would high-five each other when taking over each other's position. Mason watched Cindy deliberately move past him. She was really mad and there was nothing he could do about it, Mason thought. It was like when Brent and he had had a big fight in the summer of '95. It was a battle royal that lasted almost three weeks. But somehow this was a lot more painful, as if the stakes were higher.

Mason snatched a pass from Anita and meticulously dribbled past centre. He looked up at the clock and saw that there were only thirty seconds remaining in the first quarter. Mason knew that if he took his time bringing the ball up he could eat enough time to make this the last play of the quarter.

Coach Pollinoffsky bellowed out from his side-line kingdom, "Take your time with it. Use up the clock."

Mason yelled out to the Raptors, "Get in the open." He heard Buckley call out for a pass, even though he was covered by the Jazz like he was giving away twenty dollar bills. Out of the corner of his eye, Mason saw Anita in the open. He deliberately threw a meandering high shot that should have gotten to her high and wide so that she could run into it. But as Anita ran for it, a Jazz forward intercepted the pass and began to drive to the Raptor net, hoping for an open shot.

"Nice going, Pippin," Buckley shouted out, loud enough to embarrass Mason in front of both teams.

Mason couldn't believe he hadn't seen that coming. He put his Avivas into high gear and smoked down the court, striving to cut-off the shrewd Jazz player. Mason could hear Coach Pollinoffsky bluster, "Get back, get your man!"

Then a Jazz guard yelled out to the forward, "Slam dunk!"

They were going to slam dunk Mason's blunder right in his face! Flying at Mach .80 down the court, practically leaving jet-black tread marks on the worn hardwood floor, Mason prayed that he could pull off a defensive miracle. He managed to get within arm's length of the Jazz forward and with all the Stretch Armstrong ability he could conjure up, he made a swiping reach for the ball. SPLAT! He fell head-over-heels into the Jazz forward and they both crumpled into a ball, like two cartoon characters plummeting down the Alps on skis.

The referee blew his whistle three jagged times and carded Mason with an interference foul.

Mason slowly got to his feet and then held out his hand in a goodwill gesture to help the Jazz forward to his feet. "Sorry, man."

The Jazz player got to his feet and as he walked away said, "Where'd you learn to play b-ball, in prison?"

That comment hit Mason pretty hard. "I didn't mean to knock him over," he said to Anita and Nikki.

"I know, it just happened," Nikki said, trying to be reassuring.

After the Jazz forward nailed his two foul shots, the clock counted down from two seconds and the scoreboard let out a thunderous quarter-ending buzz.

Mason hobbled to the bench, expecting the worst from the coach. He took the last spot on the bench, sandwiched between Buckley and Rodney.

"Come on team ..." the coach searched for just the right words of encouragement. "We're only down by ten points. Basically we're doing a great job against a very tough team. If we all give it everything we have ... I bet we can make some ground in the next quarter."

Mason saw the coach look at him and expected to be used as an example of what not to do. Instead, the coach didn't utter one word. But Mason knew that the coach's look was one of those special glances that insinuated everything without him having to say anything. Mason knew he was in the coach's bad books.

"Okay boys and girls," Coach Pollinoffsky said while clapping his hands loudly, "let's make each other proud."

The break elapsed so quickly that Mason felt there was no time for him to recharge his batteries. He struggled to his feet, took one step onto the court and practically cut-off Cindy.

"Sorry," Mason said. Cindy didn't say anything. She just moved off.

Buckley snickered, "Nice going, Don Juan."

Rodney, acting as Buckley's entourage, laughed out loud.

He had to at least try talking to her, Mason thought. Scraping up some courage, he caught up to Cindy and said, "We should talk for a second."

Cindy said, "Yeah, we probably should," and walked away.

What did that mean? Mason asked himself. Was that good or bad?

Just then, the referee blew his whistle and the second quarter was on.

From the left-forward position, Mason watched Cindy take the ball and knock it toward Rodney. Mason thought that Cindy was probably being sarcastic although he was a little confused by her "Yeah, we probably should" comment.

The coach yelled out, "Go offence." Rodney bounced the ball into the three-point zone and made a cross-court pass to Buckley.

Mason reached out and intercepted the pass, trying to take control and get into the grove of the game.

"Pass it. Pass it," Buckley demanded, peeved that the ball was not in his hands.

Mason decided not to pass it and tried to hold off the Jazz long enough to spot a footpath to the net. He saw Cindy get into the open under the net and Mason knew that he had to make his move immediately. The Jazz guards applied some pressure, forcing Mason to take a step back.

"I'm in the open," Cindy yelled out to Mason.

Now she decided to talk to him, Mason thought, not understanding why he was acting so childish about their situation.

He took a step to the side while dribbling the ball and faked out the Jazz guard. Then he ploughed his weight forward, making a hard B-line for the lattice net. Steps away from the bucket he clutched the ball and took his two allowable steps toward the mesh. He spotted Cindy under the net with her hands extended, begging for the ball. Mason leapt into the air, taking flight like a super-charged, turbine-driven Boeing jet. He extended his arm toward the rim, cradling the ball in the palm of his hand. But he overcompensated and the ball ricocheted off the backboard and bounced out of bounds.

The moment that the referee sounded his whistle, Coach Pollinoffsky yelled, "Mason."

Like a dog responding to its owner, Mason chugged toward the coach.

"You had several opportunities to pass and you didn't." The coach ran his fingers through his thin, whiskered hair. "Did you or did you not see Cindy clearly in the open?" The coach didn't wait for Mason to respond and then hit with, "You're benched."

Mason immediately exclaimed a defensive "What?"

Coach Pollinoffsky commented, "You look distracted out there. Take a seat." Then he looked over to Isaac. "You're in."

Mason had nothing to say. The coach was right. Mason wanted to tell the coach that he would do better and that there was no need to pull him from the game. But he decided there was no point. Besides, he didn't want to make a big scene in front of a whole gymnasium full of people. Mason took a seat on the bench, sweating everywhere, and felt about as isolated from everything as the first astronaut must have felt on the moon.

10

Cosmic Crunch

The buzzer blasted and the Raptors came off the floor to huddle listlessly around the bench for the half-time break. They were down by eighteen points and feeling it. Mason looked at his worn-out teammates, sweat streaming from their foreheads, and felt responsible for the bad half. He couldn't believe he'd been benched. Watching his team losing and not being able to do anything about it was like watching his dreams of going to Ottawa vanish before his eyes. Not to mention that Cindy was the only thing on his mind, and she wouldn't even sit near him. When the team came off the court, Cindy positioned herself as far down the bench from Mason as possible.

Coach Pollinoffsky sauntered over to the team, clipboard in hand. Mason noticed that he was scrutinizing the team and probably calculating what to say to pep them up. "That was a very tough half," he said slowly, as if he didn't really believe it.

There were mutters of agreement from the exhausted group of players.

Then Coach Pollinoffsky looked directly at Mason and said, "I want everyone to take a few minutes and think about what you're doing out there. I've been coaching basketball long enough to know that we can beat this team. Now I want each and every one of you to concentrate and to understand that for yourselves." The coach put his clipboard down on the bench and walked off, leaving his team with something to think about.

Silence beset the bench. The only thing Mason could hear was a wall of chatter from the bleachers topped off by a high-pitched cry from a player's baby brother.

Mason decided he had to do something. He couldn't let the team down, or let himself down. He had to talk to Cindy. But how could he get through to her? The last time he tried to talk to her she shunned him. He looked down the bench and watched Cindy and Anita talking. Then he shifted his gaze across the court to the Jazz, who were strutting around their bench. They looked like a team with real confidence and not a care in the world. He could see all the players laughing and acting like they had the game in the bag. As Mason sat back, Coach Pollinoffsky's words kept bobbing around in his mind. "We can beat these guys."

He had to get proactive ... All right, Mason said to himself. Enough acting like a scaredy cat. He had to make things right. He would make it so she couldn't ignore him, he thought. He'd force the issue.

So, taking a deep breath, Mason got up, strode past his teammates and plopped himself right next to Cindy. She immediately turned her head away and left him staring at her ponytail. He cleared his throat to get her to look at him. But she kept her head turned and didn't take any notice.

"I understand how important the drinking thing is," Mason said, trying to get right into the heart of the matter.

Cindy swung her head around and stared right at him. So he didn't have to look her in the eye, he focused intently on the bench's varnish, examining every groove. But he could feel Cindy's stare pound on him. "No you don't, Mason. If you knew how important the drinking issue was then you wouldn't have had any beer," she said sternly.

He could see that this was going to be as easy as walking through a field of land mines. He had probably offended Cindy more than he had offended anyone in his whole existence.

When she spoke, her eyes got really big. "The point is, I don't know if I can ever trust you again." She took in a deep breath. "And how can we be friends if I can't trust you?"

"It's about your dad, right?" Mason asked, trying to let her know that he understood where she was coming from.

"No. It's about you." She went on, "My dad is a separate issue." She didn't let up her stare. "You disrespected me even after you knew that my dad had a problem with alcohol."

"I'm sorry," Mason said.

"Sometimes sorry just doesn't cut it," she said as she broke eye contact with him.

"But Cindy, I really am sorry. I'll never let anything like this happen again." Mason felt really bad, but he was happy that they were at least talking now. He could actually feel some of the hurt dissipate.

"I guess I know that you're sorry."

Mason sighed, somewhat relieved.

Cindy continued, "I just needed to know that you understood why what you did was wrong."

"I totally do," he remarked in a low voice, obviously upset.

There was a moment of calm between the two of them, like a tornado had just passed. Mason raised his head and looked Cindy in the eye. He managed a little smile, which she returned. Then Cindy placed her hand on Mason's back and softly patted it. For a nanosecond he felt a jolt of electricity course through his veins. This was the sign. Mason remembered Tyrone telling him that if a girl touched you in a soft way it meant that she liked you. This was the softest touch Mason had ever felt.

"So, I guess we're —"

Cindy cut him off. "Friends again? Yes."

"Now all I have to do is convince Coach Pollinoffsky that I shouldn't be benched and that I'm ready to play."

"Let me take care of that." She sprang to her feet and went over to the coach who was talking-up the ref under the scoreboard.

Mason could see Cindy explaining something. The coach was listening intently. Then the two of them walked toward the bench.

"So, Mason," the coach said as he approached with Cindy by his side. "Are you ready to play?"

Mason wasn't sure what Cindy had said to their coach. But it worked. It looked like Mason was being given another chance. "I sure am," he announced.

"Good. We really could use you out there," he said as he picked up his clipboard from its spot on the bench. Then Coach Pollinoffsky assumed an authoritative stance in front of the team. "Okay, team," he continued, "let's get out there and show them that the Raptors mean business. I want Cindy, Buckley, Mason, Nikki, and Gavin to start."

Cindy stood centre court right across from a huge Jazz player. He wasn't quite six feet tall — but close enough. Mason stood to Cindy's left and Buckley to her right.

The ref chirped his whistle to signal the start of the second half of play. Mason could feel the adrenalin coursing through his body. This was it. If the Raptors didn't completely dominate this half of the game, they would lose. To Mason that wasn't an option. He wasn't going to let a trip to Ottawa trickle through his fingers.

"Tweet." The whistle went again as the ref tossed the ball in the air above Cindy and the huge Jazz player.

Cindy got a piece of it and tipped it to the right.

It soared through the air and Buckley grabbed it and gained control. As he started to dribble up court Mason saw him signal to put on a forward press. So Mason ran up court and got in the face of the Jazz defence. Buckley snapped a pass over to Cindy who deked around a Jazz player. Then she volleyed a pass over to Mason who shot it back to her once she got in the key.

"Shoot," Mason yelled.

Cindy took the shot and ... rebound. Mason was on it. He grabbed the ball, bounced it twice then lofted an easy one, up close and personal, at the net. Two points.

As Mason and the Raptors retreated into their end, the Jazz took possession and started to make their way toward them.

Mason looked over to Cindy who looked over to Buckley. They knew what they had to do. Mason signalled Cindy to start her advance up to the Jazz' end of the court. Then he and Buckley both targeted the player with the ball and pounced on him. They caged him in and snatched the orangey globe away from him. Mason dribbled it for a beat, bounce passed it over to Buckley who shot it up court to Cindy. When Cindy got her hands on it she had a free run of the court. Mason watched with mirth as she ran down and performed a picture-perfect layup.

"Another two," Mason and Buckley yelled at the same time as they reached for a high five.

"All right," they heard the coach holler from the bench. "Way to play, team."

Mason looked up at the stands and saw his mom and Jim clapping and cheering him on. But there was no time to let his guard down. The Raptors might have scored four points really quickly but they were still down by fourteen.

Now the Jazz had possession again and they weren't going to let themselves get caged in. They spread out and came toward the Raptors chest-passing all the way. As they reached the rim of the Raptor's key they sped up their passing momentum. Mason tried to guess where the next pass was going so he could intercept. But the Jazz had been playing together a long time. They had this routine down pat.

Tyrone stood under the net in his best defensive stance. But when the Jazz decided to advance into the key the Raptors were practically defenseless against their opponents' plan of attack. Three Jazz players got under the net and confused the issue. Then they shot a pass back to the free-throw line where one of their guys caught it and swished a two-pointer.

Even the Raptors were impressed by the play. But the Jazz would not be able to do it again. There would definitely be a Raptor guarding the line next time, Mason mused.

Tyrone tossed Mason the ball. Mason started to dribble up court. He lobbed a pass up to Cindy who took an easy shot. Another two. Cindy got high fives all around.

"Nice one," Coach Pollinoffsky yelled.

As they walked back to their end, Mason turned to Buckley and Cindy. "It doesn't look like they're guarding you very closely," he said to Cindy. "I bet if we keep feeding you the ball we'll make up a lot of points."

"Good plan." The three of them agreed.

A few Jazz players were now encroaching on Raptor territory like vermin. But the guy with the ball was hanging back.

Mason knew that once his opponents had jockeyed for good positions, the guard would throw in a pass. The trick was to figure out who was going to get the pass and try to intercept it. He saw one Jazz player who seemed to be open. If he looks open to me — he'll definitely look open to the guy with the ball, Mason surmised. So Mason cut between the open player and the guard, intercepting the anticipated pass perfectly. He flew down court and slammed in an ace.

The home crowd went wild, even chanting Mason's name.

* * * * *

It was a minute away from the end of the game. After a great Raptor comeback, the score was tied at forty-six.

The home team was now on the defensive as the Jazz quickly approached. Each Raptor was guarding a man. Mason danced around a kid who had flaming red hair. The kid was trying desperately to get away. But Mason was sticking to him like fungus. Earlier in the game Mason had heard one of the other Jazz players call this guy Steam Roller. From his size alone Mason could figure out why. Steam Roller could probably drive through an entire team to get in position for the perfect shot. That's exactly what he's trying to do now, Mason thought. He was definitely going to be receiving a pass. Sure enough the minute Mason let down his guard, the ball came sailing over to his end and landed right in Steam Roller's hands. But Mason wasn't going to let him take a shot. As Steam Roller raised his hands, Mason got in next to him and tipped his arm.

TWEET. "Foul." The ref yelled.

Steam Roller now had two free shots on net and Mason was feeling like General Custer.

Mason stood along the key, next to the grizzly Jazz player. Across from him, Tyrone stood next to another Jazz player and next to that player was Nikki. Everyone stood still as Steam Roller bounced the ball at the foul line. Mason prayed that he wouldn't make the shot. The opposing player lifted up the ball slowly then aimed and ... swoosh. Nothing but net.

This was not good. The Raptors were down by one with slightly less than a minute to go. Mason felt his heart sink. They hadn't made this kind of comeback only to lose by a single point.

The ref tossed Steam Roller the ball for his second shot. Everyone around the net knew that no matter what happened there would only be time for one or two more plays once the free throw punishment was over. The big kid bounced the ball once, lifted it to his head, aimed, and missed. There was a scramble for the ball.

"I got it," Tyrone yelled.

Most of the Jazz scampered to get positioned defensively as Tyrone whipped a pass over to Nikki.

Mason looked to the ball. He saw a Jazz player slowly advancing in on Nikki. "Watch out," he warned.

The Jazz player quickly snuck in and plucked the ball right from under her.

"Noooo," Mason yelled as the Jazz player ran down to attempt the slam. He felt helpless as the player went in at full steam. But what neither the Jazz nor the Raptors had counted on was the defensive skills of Tyrone. Just as the Jazz player went for the shot, Tyrone howled in. With incredible skill he tricked the Jazz player out and stole the ball right from his hands.

"It's coming uptown," Tyrone yelled as he took his best quarterback stance and lobbed the ball as far as he could.

Mason watched the ball sail over his head. He ran to meet it at its landing spot. As he grabbed it he was immediately confronted by two Jazz players.

"Ten seconds," he heard coach Pollinoffsky yell.

Mason saw that Cindy was open so he scratched off a pass that just reached her. Then the Jazz players left his zone to gang up on her. This gave Mason the time he needed to get in close to the hoop. Cindy must have seen the Jazz coming because in a flash she fed the ball off to Buckley. Buckley then took a shot. Rebound. Mason lept for it. He had the ball. The game was all his. He jumped in the air as high as he could and SLAM DUNK — he got it in.

Just then, the *wahhhh* of the game-ending buzzer sounded.

"We win!" Mason heard Buckley yell.

Everyone in the stands went wild. The Raptors had come back from an eighteen-point deficit to win the game by one.

Cindy ran up to Mason and wrapped her arms around him in an excited hug. Mason loved being that close to her. "We did it," she yelled. She let go and they gave each other a high five.

"We did it," he shouted. "Now we really have a shot at going to Ottawa."

As they smiled at each other the rest of the team gathered around. Everyone was cheering at the top of their lungs. What a victory.

11

Sub Zero

"So, kid ... what'll it be?" A gruff, middle-aged man wearing a white apron and paper serving hat asked Mason. Then he dunked his ice cream scooper into a metallic basin full of water and swished it around.

Mason could see the remnants of whatever was left on the scooper dissolve into the water. He looked up at the long list of flavours hanging behind the man and thought about what he was going to have. Rocky road? Naw, too rich for a post game treat, he thought. He needed something to quench his thirst while maximizing flavour.

"What are you getting, Mason?" Cindy asked, standing elbow-to-elbow with him, staring at the brightly coloured flavour catalog.

"I'm not sure," he said. "I was thinking about chocolate but I'll probably just go with pralines 'n' cream. It's always been my favourite. How about you?"

"Double chocolate mint bubble gum," she said, proud of her originality.

"Wow. Cool flavour."

Then the ice-cream man barked at Mason again, "Look, kid, you're holding up the line."

Mason gave a quick glance over his shoulder. The entire team, his mom and Jim were standing there waiting.

"Pralines 'n' cream," Mason ordered.

"And I'll have the double chocolate mint bubble gum," Cindy added.

Mason watched as the man's thick, grey-haired arms reached into the tub of ice cream and bore into the creamy-brown substance. The ice cream rolled easily into the scooper, like a tidal wave crashing down on itself, creating a perfect ball. Then the man placed the frozen globe on top of a sugar cone.

"That'll be a buck fifty," he said.

Jim moved to the front of the line. "I'll be covering the whole group of them," he said to the ice-cream man.

The players all looked up and said in unison, "Thanks."

"Don't mention it," Jim said with a smile. "You all deserve it for playing so well. That was probably the best comeback in the history of your school." Then Jim rejoined Patricia at the back of the line.

Mason and Cindy got their ice-cream cones and went to sit down at an orange, plastic bench in the back of the little parlour. Mason was as happy as he could remember. He thought to himself how glad he was that Cindy was here and that they were friends again.

"I can't believe we played so well in the last half," Mason said.

"You turned the game around totally. Everyone else was inspired by you," Cindy complimented.

"Yeah," Tyrone added as he took a seat while trying to stop his double-scoop almond-fudge from dripping. "Whatever you did, it worked."

Mason was starting to feel flush, absorbing the compliments. He tried to brush them off and said, "I don't know. Everyone really worked together." Don't get too delirious, he told himself. They are just acting this way because we won. Isaac sat down and started to eat spoonfuls of ice cream from his plastic container, necessary because he was allergic cones.

"Ashbury, nice to see you didn't blow it in the second ha like you did in the first," Buckley said as he walked past wit his ice-cream cone in hand.

Even Buckley was almost complimenting him, Mason realized. He'd better write that one down for the record book!

"Yeah, thank's Buckley," Mason said.

Mason was still thinking about what a hassle it had been to get Buckley and the other guys to play with the girls. As well, he couldn't wrap his mind around the fact that Buckley had almost completely destroyed his relationship with Cindy by offering him the beer.

As Buckley was about to sit down at another bench he said, "And Ashbury, you were right about playing as a team."

Mason couldn't believe what he was hearing as he finished off his cone. That was as close as he would ever come to hearing Buckley admit that he was wrong.

Buckley went on, "If we continue to play this way for the rest of the season, we can't lose."

"He's right," Cindy said as she chomped down on the remnants of her sugar cone. "We are looking really good. Just imagine what we'll be like if we get to practise more."

She had a point, Mason thought, pumped with optimism. He imagined what the team would be like after more time together. They would be able to anticipate each other's moves, making the big plays by using telepathic communication.

"Seriously," Tyrone remarked, "when we get some routines down, we'll kick."

It was at that moment Mason knew that the Cabbagetown Raptors had the ability to go all the way. It would be a struggle, he thought. But at least now they'd go out fighting.

12

Life on Mars

Mason stood outside staring at a battered, old basketball net on its last thread, hanging from the rim. He held a basketball in his hand, then started to dribble it on the same spot over and over, in some sort of trance. He focused on the barely recognizable red square on the backboard. If anyone walked by they'd think Mason was a kid completely possessed. But in actuality he had never in his life been more focused. The January air was damp and frigid. Mason could feel his puffs of breath crystallize in front of his mouth. He continued to pound the ball into precisely the same spot on the pavement. The sound of the cold basketball echoing against the frozen asphalt was as consistent as a pulse. Mason's left hand was jealous that his right hand got to do all the work. Look at me, Mason thought, standing here in the nation's capital. Who'd ever have thought he'd finally get to go to Ottawa.

The rest of the regular season had gone really well for the Raptors. They managed to fend off any losses despite some very close brushes with defeat. Nonetheless, the guys and girls had managed to spark a cohesiveness in the early season that carried them, victory after victory, to Ottawa. The best part of all was that Mason had been able to spend some quality time in Ottawa with his best friend, Brent. All the hard work had paid off.

Life on Mars

Mason continued to bounce the ball amidst trees la[den] with icicles. His left hand began to feel the icy perils of [the] cold Ottawa winter, while the right hand fought off the col[d]ness by busying itself with the basketball. It was time for [a] slam dunk. Mason dug his right foot into the ground and pushed the ball forward. He followed the gravity-suppressed path of the ball as his momentum propelled him forward like a snowball. With the tangled mesh of the outdoor court's net in perspective he cut into the air, taking off. Once Mason was high in the sky, he began to drive the ball with the velocity only two hands could provide. The ball drilled a path through the hoop and Mason landed with the agility of a cat back on earth.

"Nice slam dunk," Cindy said out of thin air.

Mason turned his attention from the successful bucket to Cindy. "Were you watching the whole time?"

"Maybe," Cindy said with just the right amount of grin to make her answer ambiguous. She walked closer to him as the basketball rolled off the perimetre of the court as though it had a mind of its own.

"Can you believe we're here?" Mason asked.

"I was just about to say the same thing." Cindy continued, "I'm really looking forward to the championship game today."

"Me too," Mason replied. "So you think we're gonna win?"

"If you had asked me that same question when I first met you my answer would have been no. But looking back at what we've gone through to get here, my answer is absolutely, definitely, indubitably — YES!"

"Cool," he said and reached out to high-five her. But this high five was different. Neither of them let go. Their hands stuck together and their fingers interlocked as though they were sewn together.

aving a great time hanging out with you,"

" Mason responded in his coolest possible tone above James Bond.

nk we get along really well."

e too," Mason repeated. He got that feeling in his . The same feeling he'd had on their first date when they yed mini golf under the picture-perfect autumn night. The me was right to take their relationship to the next level, Mason thought. Before his confidence subsided, he leaned in and gave Cindy a kiss on the lips.

Time stood still.

It was as though the third dimension cracked apart giving birth to some warped looking fourth dimension — where even breathing seemed exponentially peculiar. While processing the experience, Mason quickly determined that his first kiss had gone off without a hitch. Cindy pulled back and gave Mason the warmest smile. He knew he had done the right thing.

Other books you'll enjoy in the Sports Stories series

Baseball

Curve Ball by John Danakas
Tom Poulos is looking forward to a summer of baseball in Toronto until his mother puts him on a plane to Winnipeg.

Baseball Crazy by Martyn Godfrey
Rob Carter wins an all-expenses-paid chance to be batboy at the Blue Jays' spring training camp in Florida.

Basketball

Slam Dunk by Steven Barwin and Gabriel David Tick
In this sequel to *Roller Hockey Blues*, Mason Ashbury's basketball team adjusts to the arrival of some new players: girls.

Camp All-Star by Michael Coldwell
In this insider's view of a basketball camp, Jeff Lang encounters some unexpected challenges.

Fast Break by Michael Coldwell
Moving from Toronto to small-town Nova Scotia was rough, but when Jeff makes the school basketball team he thinks things are looking up.

Nothing but Net by Michael Coldwell
The Cape Breton Grizzly Bears face an out-of-town basketball tournament they're sure to lose.

Figure Skating

A Stroke of Luck by Kathryn Ellis
Strange accidents are stalking one of the skaters at the Millwood Arena.

Gymnastics

The Perfect Gymnast by Michele Martin Bossley
Abby's new friend has all the confidence she lacks, but she also has a serious problem that nobody but Abby seems to know about.

by John Danakas
...ger on the thirteen-year-old Transcona Sharks adjusts ...oest friend and his mom's boyfriend.

...ight in Transcona by John Danakas
...y Powell gets promoted to the Transcona Sharks' first line, ...mping out the coach's son who's not happy with the change.

...e Off by Chris Forsyth
A talented hockey player finds himself competing with his best friend for a spot on a select team.

Hat Trick by Jacqueline Guest
The only girl on an all-boys' hockey team works to earn the captain's respect and her mother's approval.

Two Minutes for Roughing by Joseph Romain
As a new player on a tough Toronto hockey team, Les must fight to fit in.

Riding

Riding Scared by Marion Crook
A reluctant new rider struggles to overcome her fear of horses.

Katie's Midnight Ride by C.A. Forsyth
An ambitious barrel racer finds herself without a horse weeks before her biggest rodeo.

A Way With Horses by Peter McPhee
A young Alberta rider invited to study show jumping at a posh local riding school uncovers a secret.

Glory Ride by Tamara L. Williams
Chloe Anderson fights memories of a tragic fall for a place on the Ontario Young Riders' Team.

Roller hockey
Roller Hockey Blues by Steven Barwin and
Gabriel David Tick
Mason Ashbury faces a summer of boredom until he makes tl roller-hockey team.

Sailing
Sink or Swim by William Pasnak
Dario can barely manage the dog paddle but thanks to his mother he's spending the summer at a water sports camp.

Soccer
Lizzie's Soccer Showdown by John Danakas
When Lizzie asks why the boys and girls can't play together, she finds herself the new captain of the soccer team.

Swimming
Breathing Not Required by Michele Martin Bossley
An eager synchronized swimmer works hard to be chosen for a solo and almost loses her best friend in the process.

Taking a Dive by Michele Martin Bossley
Josie holds the provincial record for the butterfly but in this sequel to *Water Fight* she can't seem to match her own time and might not go on to the nationals.

Water Fight! By Michele Martin Bossley
Josie's perfect sister is driving her crazy but when she takes up swimming — Josie's sport — it's too much to take.

PRINTED AND BOUND
IN BOUCHERVILLE, QUÉBEC, CANADA
BY MARC VEILLEUX IMPRIMEUR INC.
IN MARCH, 1998